I0682448

WHAT REMAINED OF KATRINA

A novel of New Orleans

Also by Kelly Jameson:

Dead On

Shards of Summer

Spellbound

Across A Dark Highland Shore

To Tame a Rogue

Desperate, Disturbed, Deranged, & Double-Lattéd

WHAT REMAINED OF KATRINA

A novel of New Orleans

by

Kelly Jameson

Swallow Tail Press

This new edition is a revised and expanded version of *What Remained of Katrina: A Novel of New Orleans*, first published in paperback and ebook formats in 2012.

Text copyright © 2012, © 2015 by Kelly Jameson
All Rights Reserved

Published by Swallow Tail Press
Philadelphia, PA, USA
www.swallowtailpress.com

ISBN-10: 0988918137
ISBN-13: 978-0-9889181-3-9

Cover photograph courtesy of Shutterstock.com

This is a work of fiction. Names, characters, places and incidents either are the product of the author's imagination or are used fictitiously. Any resemblance to actual persons, living or dead, events, incidents or locales is entirely coincidental.

Dedicated to all the artists to come.

Part I

1

You sit across the street, slouched over the wheel, in dark glasses and a blonde wig. Not much of a disguise, you know, but adequate for what you need to pull off. It's all about illusion. Think about it. Where does a play take place? On a stage? No, you corrugated lame ass. In the mind of the observer. Magic and showmanship. Psychology and illusion. Art and art making. Forcing viewers to interpret what they see in ways they know are fake is as close to real magic as all of us sewage farts are likely to get.

You watch as pathetic, unfathomably moronic people from all walks of life pay respects to your former bad self, Katrina Lalande Jones Thomas Jackson Miller. A black American, married four times, divorced three, a registered Independent with a string of unrelated and forgettable careers, and your token nightmarish childhood.

Take the time, for example, your bio Dad took you to get a double-dip ice cream cone, and like the loser you were, you dropped it on the sidewalk outside a bus station. You were the kind of kid who was so poor you bent down, scooped it off the germ-infested concrete with your hammy paws, and ate it anyway. You fold up your hands like a sagging tent. Let us pray.

Telling people you had Tourette's so you could swear righteously in public. One or two convictions for public lewdness. Don't look at the face, folks. Look at the wrist. There is nothing up your sleeve. No strings. No tricks.

Broke most of your life, your passive-aggressive self liked to eat in cheap chicken joints and sit in empty churches. You never went to church when it was full of people. You didn't believe in that.

Here's a neat trick folks. You nearly drowned in the second story bedroom of a neighbor you wanted to bone during the worst catastrophe on American soil. Oh, and you thought you were Vincent van Gogh reincarnated. A Dutch Post-Impressionist painter who shot himself to death in the Year of Our Lord 1890. Who, during his short life, shared a yellow house in the South of France for nine weeks with leading Post-Impressionist painter Paul Gauguin.

Of course it only makes sense that you believe you were Van Gogh. People who remember past lives are always someone famous, aren't they? Nobody ever remembers being a syphilitic, wart-covered whore with three teeth or someone who shepherded turds through the inner workings of a local sewer plant.

Van Gogh, or you when you were Van Gogh, didn't pick up a paintbrush until he was thirty. He, or you when you were Van Gogh, produced most of his work in twenty-nine months of frenzied, robust activity. Eight hundred or so paintings and roughly the same number of drawings. Eight hundred.

One hundred years after Van Gogh's, or your, ignoble, self-inflicted, nearly botched death by revolver, a painting he did of his friend, Dr. Gachet, sold for over $82 million. You couldn't sell it while you were alive. Van Gogh's, or your, work is now owned by every major art museum in the world. Ain't posthumous fame a bitch?

But you weren't exactly the poster child for tortured genius, were you? You hadn't painted anything since you were a teenager. But like when you were Van Gogh, you continued to notice the rampant sexuality of arbuscles, hedges, and treelets; the scarlet, gold-green flecks of nature; the sun slipping down the other side of the blue heavens; stars and skies that made you want to dream.

You possessed a daring classification of music and faith, believing in God in the big-picture sense, Mozart, Beethoven, and Thelonious Monk. You understood double entendre and dysphemism. How many people can say that? You believe you noticed things, little things, other people didn't and maybe that was true. You were used to being ignored and disliked. So, those are a few good things they can say about you anyway.

When you were twelve, almost thirteen, you started having vivid dreams you couldn't explain. Dreams of a being a Dutch Post-Impressionist painter with a shock of red-orange hair who cut off his own ear. Van Gogh probably had a good reason for cutting off his ear. He'd fallen in love with a teenage prostitute who had, on more than one occasion, maybe after he fucked her or she sucked him off, told him how much she loved his pink ears. In fact, if he was ever strapped for cash, she told him she would be delighted to have one of his cute little pink ears as payment. That's reasonable. I mean, who wouldn't cut his ear off in that situation?

So, you dreamt you were a beige ribbon of beach, a curl of silver crescent moon, a musket and lobe of stars. You saw yourself, a white man, ugly and angular and bony looking, staring into a mirror, the same one you painted your own portrait in many times. Your syphilitic-red eyes and craggy brow reflected back at you. You took a razor, licked your dry lips as you felt its sharp tongue against your white flesh, calmly slashed off part of your right ear, leaving only a portion of the lobe.

You wrapped your partial ear in drawing paper. Tied it in a bundle of newspaper. Haphazardly pulled a dark beret over your head, over your wound, fibers sticking in the blood. Went out. Gave your ear to Rachel the teenage prostitute. Naturally. Of course. She fainted. You walked away. Well, she was kind of a bitch anyway.

Now that you're gone, cunt lips, maybe the world will finally understand what you have tried to say in this place of submerged lifetimes and pernicious beauty.

As you, a lovely magician's assistant with too much cellulite on your thighs and a penchant for Category 5 American Pale Ale, are sawed in half during your watery, way-too-conspicuous mid-life crisis, you wonder if you can have a volunteer from the audience. No? No one steps up? Well then, when you are done being sawed in half, you hope at least they give you a hand.

2

You adjust your sunglasses as you watch your own funeral and then you realize you have a wedgie. Before you came to your own funeral service, you were looking at the TV news, listening to a blonde lady in a red power suit with matching red power lipstick tell you how to cut your grocery bill in half. And you were eating Cheesy Cheddar BBQ Cheetos. Which you washed down with a cold Category 5 American Pale Ale. There's a part of you that loves chili cheese Fritos and the crunchy goodness of Cheetos. Well combine the two and that's what you get when you open up a bag of Cheesy Cheddar BBQ Cheetos. No matter what that stanky ass bitch TV news anchor says, you're not cutting back on BBQ Cheetos or Category 5 American Pale Ale. It's a flavor explosion that goes perfectly with a sandwich or a burger and can even stand alone as a wonderful breakfast, as you've aptly demonstrated. Not to mention that the pale ale pours a light amber color with about a half finger of white head and moderate lacing, and who doesn't need that first thing in the morning?

He makes me lie down in green pastures; He leads me beside quiet waters.

You were a vocal scatting, a well-articulated piano solo, jazz-pop style, a contrapuntal melodic presentation, Katrina-who-thought-she-was-Van-Gogh. You catch yourself tearing up. You had your good points.

The day started with your memorial service and funeral in your native New Orleans. Your wishes were that you be cremated. You didn't want your coffin and corpse floating outta your crypt at the next heavy rain, everybody seeing your big, bloated business. Happens all too often around here, especially after Katrina.

You'd been a lot of things in life—a failed hooker, a hotel maid, a magician's assistant in the French Quarter, even drove an ice cream truck for a while.

You watch now as an ice cream truck leads the funeral procession, beginning at Poydras and St. Charles and winds slowly through the Quarter. Bands play; chunks of trombone notes noodle the air; people dance and wiggle. Hookers and aproned owners of Lucky Dog hotdog stands look on without much interest. A few preppy college students with cotton-candy–colored cocktails flat out ignore it. The ever-present palm readers, magicians, street musicians, and mimes conduct their business and drink their native chicory coffee, offended by Starbucks.

Maybe it's not exactly the same now, but truth is, while other neighborhoods were annihilated, the Quarter was largely untouched by Katrina's rage. But people didn't know that because all they saw on the news were flooded streets everywhere. In the Quarter, you can still eat your way to the US mint and back. You know all about that.

If you have a hankering to learn more about America's Worst Catastrophe, you can take a New Orleans bus tour, experience an eyewitness account of the events surrounding the most devastating disaster on American soil, all from your big, fat-ass bus seat for about forty bucks. You can take pictures of your friends standing next to the leaning and buckled homes where Dads trying to rescue their little kids failed, and families all drowned together in the toxic black waters of the Mississippi. The tour travels through ravaged neighborhoods like Lakeview, Gentilly, New Orleans East, and the Ninth Ward. Ghost towns now. But not like they have out west, with tumbleweeds and dust and shit. Watery ghost towns. I mean, you shouldn't have to watch the tide roll in in your own neighborhood, right?

You make your way toward water and a field with trees shaped like bent old women, wind brushing the tree moss with its antique dreams.

You didn't want to be cremated and shot from a cannon's mouth; those types of funereal spectacles aren't you. You did your research when you married Ray. What were you thinking when you did that? About purchasing a huge chrome rhino head with a hollow horn for your cremated remains and an urn that plays "How Dry I Am" when opened. That's what you were thinking.

You also thought, you know, it might be cool to have your ashes launched into space like Gene Roddenberry supposedly did, but only rich people can afford that kind of thing. Plus, it seems lonely to you. And kind of like littering. In 1991, Roddenberry's ashes were supposedly sent into space in a capsule the size of a lipstick tube to orbit Earth for just over five years, and then they burned up in Earth's atmosphere.

You thought about buying a Google map and GPS coordinates to help people find the exact spot where your ashes would be scattered, but that seemed geeky. And unnatural. Plus, the commercial companies you checked out charge about three hundred fifty bucks for an aerial burial that assures dignity and legality. You weren't interested in one without dignity and legality. But unless somebody goes along on the flight, how do you know they aren't just dumping your queef-cake ashes over a vacant lot or a McDonald's playground where someone was raped or a toxic landfill? Or worse, how do you know they even scatter them at all? After all, you're dead, aren't you? So you should care.

You'd heard of people ordering specially made caskets, like a beer bottle-shaped coffin for an irreverent drinker or a coffin shaped like a hotdog for a pork lover, complete with replica mustard and roll, but like you said, you didn't want a coffin made from hardwoods cut down from dank rain forests and shipped halfway around the world just to end up in the damp, disarmed ground. And no way you were gonna be buried in something that looked like a giant hotdog.

Now you realize that things like nitrogen oxide, sulfur oxide, and carbon monoxide are given off by cremation processes, and some people are freaked out about mercury released into the environment when dead people with lots of mercury fillings in their teeth are burned up, but you figured it was the lesser of two sizzling evils.

Turns out all this didn't matter much anyhow, as all that was left of you after the storm was your left hand. Yep, that's right. Your left hand. Because you couldn't stop thinking about your neighbor, the one you wanted to bone, the one next door.

3

Your best friend in life, Mary, flips on the music in the ice cream truck and scans through the thirty-two options trying to find a tune she likes that will annoy everyone within earshot. She's dressed in a deep rose-colored blouse and dark skirt and cheap silver jewelry. Earrings sparkle on her ears. She knows blasting an annoying tune would make you happy. While you never really knew how to be comfortable on the planet, you were comfortable with people not liking you.

She settles on "It's a Small World After All" and the tune begins to tinkle-drift-pound like a bad headache from the loudspeakers into the hot, soggy, chin-scratching morning.

"It sounds cheerful enough," you hear her say, as she creeps along at about seven miles per hour, nervously twisting a braid of her hair in her hand, making her way to where they will finally scatter your pudgy little fingers of dust.

There used to be ice cream trucks everywhere. Not that you ever made much use of them. They didn't offer ice cream in Cuban cigar flavor or Captain Morgan flavor. Some people are real bastards.

All of the guests—except for the strippers of course—are in their pajamas. You were pretty specific about your last wishes. There are about three hundred people here. They look pretty comfortable. Douche bags have been known to add small numbers with calculators and call it "business math." Three hundred people all here to honor you. If you do the "business math."

You watch as the ice cream truck parks on an edge of the field that seems to be melting in the heat. Soon everyone is chomping on popsicles, Fudgesicles, Rocket Pops, Creamsicles, and those Spiderman pops with their unseeing, white-sugar–gumball eyes. That's love... that's life... the purple-orange-pink-white mess of melting popsicle dripping down someone's stupid chin.

Strippers clad in bikinis gyrate, their hips curved and alive beneath the fat blue sky and the stark trees. What's left of the trees. In China, large crowds at a funeral are a sign of honor.

To pump up the number of mourners, relatives often hire strippers to perform at funerals. This makes sense to you, as does the reasoning that people are more likely to attend funerals if leopard-print panties are tossed at them. Let us pray. But first, please take a moment to remove the underwear from your heads.

You watch as a stripper strokes the chest of a man and he joins her in dancing. You think it's one of your ex-husbands. You were married four times. But don't worry; Brigham Young, that Mormon leader, was married nineteen times. And Prophet Muhammad twelve, including to a nine-year-old. Kind of makes Liz Taylor's eight trips down the aisle look sort of pathetic in comparison. And even Louis Armstrong was only married six times. Once maybe even to his trumpet. So don't be such a loser. At least none of your relationships ended with you delivering your severed ear to someone who'd admired it during a passionless, choreographed, stinky, disease-ridden sex act.

Funny thing, that. Getting married. For each member of the marriage, it's not a talisman against falling in love with someone other than your spouse. Bad divorces don't keep you from falling in love again either. Funny that. Diego fell in love a lot while you were married. Penny, a flatulent, handsome Caucasian and ex-baseball player, fell in love with a petite blonde ten years younger than you; ironically, she worked at a Wash Out Laundromat. George got arrested for riding his bicycle naked and drunk and skipping out on child support payments to several other wives he was still in love with. George needed to reject people before they rejected him. Maybe that's why he rode his bicycle naked and drunk, so he could reject society before it rejected him. Ray flirted a lot with a tall, skinny black woman who had bruised fingertips from practicing her jazz violin so much, but she was in love with her violin and Ray just didn't get it. Who can say what love is or what it means? One thing it ain't is perfect or explainable.

It's months after Katrina now; they never did find the rest of your body. The post-Katrina police force is spread a little thin. Hundreds and hundreds are missing. Still. So Mary finally talked Ray into having this memorial service for you.

You watch dark Negro women like your former self lick bone-colored ice cream while they dance barefoot beneath cones of blue sky. The pink soles of their feet are a vivid contrast to the grass. You hear them say things about your crybaby life. You hear them laugh, some cry, some don't say anything but you don't want to listen too closely right now anyway; you don't want to hear your dirty little life revealed and remembered in the deep, wet puddles of their mouths.

You want people to remember some of the things you loved: Saturday morning cartoons, art supplies, laughing loudly and a lot, passionate kisses, story-telling, penny licorice, sticky melting ice cream on your paws—not the gimmicky tattletales of cemeteries.

You tap your chewed red fingernails on the dashboard of your newly acquired, classic, used red Caddy (which no one will recognize as yours), potato chip crumbs on the seat next to you, salt on your lips. You rev the engine. Good and loud. The open road calls. Good and loud. But the future is hard to see, and like that ice cream on the sidewalk, a little harder to lick off your fingers.

4

You decide to park on an edge of the field, under the shade of a magnolia, its broad, fingered leaves creating a lace of cobwebbed shadows. Perfect cover for your Caddy. No one pays you or your red boat-of-a-car any mind, and this way, you can hear people talk about you. Because now you're kind of curious.

"I can't believe all that was left of her was her left hand," you hear someone say to Mary.

Mary looks puzzled, like she doesn't know what to say. No one ever knows what to say at a funeral, do they? "Do you want a Spiderman Pop?" she asks.

Soon the tired, thin ashes of your left hand drift noncommittally across the shores of the lake. No launching into space. No hotdog-shaped container. No blasting of cannons. No business cards with GPS coordinates for finding the ashes of Katrina's left hand. Although it would be kind of cool to have a small card to give away with a graphic of a hand giving everyone the finger. Something for people to remember you by. That'd be a nice note to go out on. Everybody's so suck-ass serious these days.

"Would it be wrong to mix the cremated remains of an ex-wife in a beer and chug it?" This question from your first husband, Diego.

"You mean like your ex-wife Katrina?" Mary answers.

"Yeah," he says and smiles, his teeth like chipped piano keys. In the heat, his lips glisten with promises. He has a handful of ex-wives and strings of halter-topped, shorty-shorts girlfriends. Probably because of those lips. He can't keep them off women. "It'd be like having one last drink with her," he says, and belches.

Mary mops sweat from her brow and her doughty face. "It ain't 'bout right or wrong, Diego. It's 'bout karma. She'd give you the runs for sure."

Diego, your first but not your worst husband, laughs. Penny, your second husband, is drunk on the floor of the ice cream truck, and Mary has to step over him to get at the popsicles. His real name is Epentus, but everyone calls him Penny. Sleeping right through his life, Epentus is. Probably one reason it didn't work out between you. It's generally helpful if both people are awake during the marriage. Plus, it's generally a mistake to marry a man with a girl's name.

Penny's sleepy, inebriated voice rises from the floor of the ice cream truck. "She thought she was Van Gogh reincarnated."

Diego shades his eyes with his beefy hand and peers into the truck. "Van Gogh? All I know 'bout Van Gogh is he cut his damn ear off." Then he belches. Then Penny belches. Then somebody asks for a Nutty Buddy bar.

"They don't make Nutty Buddy bars anymore," Mary says. "They're not produced commercially in large numbers across the US. That makes me sad as hell. The former manufacturer was the Sweetheart Cup Company, which also manufactured the machines that produced the cones; Sweetheart went out of business in 1998. One of the last manufacturers of the Nutty Buddy is Purity Dairies, but they're in Nashville." Nobody says anything.

Husband number three, George, walks up. "Can I get me a SpongeBob pop with the gumball reward?" George is on house arrest; he has an ankle brace on that tracks his movements. For once, he is wearing clothing. Out of respect for your dead self. You guess he doesn't get a lot of popsicles these days. "Sure, George," Mary says.

"You know, Van Gogh woulda had trouble painting a Nutty Buddy. Kat said he—or she when she was him—had trouble with red-brown combinations." Mary gives him a SpongeBob pop.

George unwraps it, takes a big bite outta SpongeBob's head. "Does SpongeBob have ears?"

"Probably not," Mary says. "He's a sponge."

"That guy Van Gogh cut his own ear off, man. Wonder what ever happened to that ear?" No one says anything, all of them standing around an ice cream truck at your funeral thinking about Van Gogh's severed ear.

Raymond walks up and says, "Who died?" and laughs. Nobody else laughs. "Yeah, she used to talk about that shit, painting, but I told her, what's the point? She'd talk about how Van Gogh liked certain colors together, like blue and yellow, which made each other shine, or some shit, that completed each other, like a man and a woman. And she said she knew that because she was Van Gogh. I told her, shit, she wasn't no Van Gogh."

Raymond was your fourth, the worst husband. He's a sneaky, mean-mouthed chorus of unforgiving muscle strung over some of the hardest bones in the city. Plus, his feet stink something almighty. He's a rutabaga-eating, crucifer-root maggot if you ever saw one.

"She used to tell people Paul Gauguin was her roommate in another lifetime and that she ran after Paul with a razor before she cut off her own ear. She was fuckin' crazy," Ray went on.

"No she wasn't," Mary said. "I mean, who's to say she *wasn't* Van Gogh? She was a great painter. I saw some of the paintings she did when she was a teenager. And they were brilliant. I don't know why she ever stopped painting. She held on to a few of them over the years. Sometimes she'd stare at them for hours. 'What are you doing?' I'd ask her. 'What do you see?' she'd ask me. I saw trees, lakes, sunflowers, shit like that. 'Look again,' she'd say. Finally she told me, underneath was the first portrait she ever did. A portrait of her bio Dad, um, in this life. He abandoned her when she was twelve, so she had to paint it from memory."

Mary frowned. "She said she remembered when she was Van Gogh, remembered painting over a lot of other paintings. Painting over early works, rejected works, and sometimes just because new canvases cost too much. And her brother Theo was sometimes late in sending them."

"Kat was a little whacked," George says. This from a man who rode his bicycle while naked and intoxicated. Then he gets a look in his eyes like he's having an actual thought and it hurts. "Van Gogh cut his ear off. Kat's hand was cut off during the flood. That's really freaky."

"Or you could say her whole body was cut off from her hand," Penny says.

"Yeah," Diego says. "You could say that. I guess. Or Van Gogh cut his whole body off from his ear."

"Anyway," Mary says, "She was really good at painting the scruffy urban edge of things, like Van Gogh, so who's to say?" Then she goes back to see how many Fudgesicles are left and so no one will see the water flooding her eyes.

"Maybe she was Van Gogh," Penny says. "Sometimes she was so stubborn her persistence was *disgusting*." This from a man who lay intoxicated on the floor of an ice cream truck.

Mary, twisting her short brown neck to look over her shoulder at Ray, says, "Nobody really knows what happened to Kat. But something or *somebody* sliced off her hand."

"Maybe she cut off her own fucking hand," Ray says. "Give me a Fudgesicle while you're back there."

"Gee Ray, looks like we're fresh out."

"Bitch. Guess I'll get Van Gogh-ing then," he says and walks away to rejoin the strippers.

Mary trudges to the front of the truck. She unwraps a Fudgesicle and starts to eat it. "You know what Kat used to say all the time? Everything's an echo. A memory. Something seen by somebody else before you see it."

You watch Ray walk away and realize how good a friend Mary was. You got plans for Ray though. That loser. He's dancing with his third stripper when you get out of the car and wander over to a dwarfish group of people clustered around the farthest edge of the field. Apparently, they don't want to get too close to you, even in death. They wouldn't notice you anyway, even though you're an explosion of brilliant colors with extremely agitated outlines.

They're alternately crying, laughing, and hugging each other. Well, mostly Ray and the stripper are hugging each other. In New Orleans, a funeral is just another excuse for a party. There have been way too many parties lately.

"Suga, I can't believe you lost your woman that way, to the storm, and then a neighbor found her hand in the driveway next door," the stripper purrs, running her fingers down his muscled forearms. "It's creepy." She pauses and strokes his hand. "You have very nice hands."

"It sure was a shock," he says, staring at her tits, and you want to bust him up bad. "Losin' her that way. Imagine. A neighbor finding her fucking hand in the driveway. It was hell, it was hell," he adds, and stuffs a crumpled dollar in her G-string. Cheap bastard.

"The police didn't find any more of her?" the stripper asks.

"Police? I didn't call no police. Why would I do that? They too busy eatin' Cheez Whiz outta their trailers. There was nothin' left of my house or Katrina, except for that hand, so I left there and never went back."

The police didn't find any more of you. Missing. Unaccounted for. Omitted. Gone. Absent. Dismissed. Cut off. Trod on. That's you.

You slide back into your Caddy and close the door with a delicate click. The red-and-white interior throws silky whispers at you; the white seat squeaks and dips beneath your serious badonkadonk ass cheeks. The 1959 beast, replete with bird droppings on its roof, speaks so eloquently of the woman behind its wheel, of her high level of personal achievement and fine sense of taste.

After your service is all over and done with, it starts to rain. You flick on the wipers with your right hand and drive away. *Thump. Thump.* You are the last to leave. The field is a lone heartbeat, emptied now of its strippers and mourners and ice cream truck and pajama'd corpses. A cathedral of drippy, wooden popsicle sticks pokes toward the sky from a large, stinky receptacle.

You feel yourself flowing back toward the sea like the floodwaters, falling in love all over again with this submerged place, the contented face of the sugared moon, with ornery, muscular men with brandy eyes, powdered apple tarts and 'po boys, dampness and shadows and lightning storms, tacky lawn ornaments, fat rain drops, tail fins, crab cakes, your fat pants, flip-flops, a man's strong hands and soft lips, raw ersters, stupid movies, blue sky, asphalt, French Toast and friends.

You cross two states before you park the Caddy and have dinner in Atlanta, Georgia as someone else.

5

You look at your good arm and think you've never seen anything more powerful than your dark, feminine skin.

You watch tendons flex as you dig into miniature beef pies, sausage rolls, sausages on sticks, cheese and olives on sticks, chicken drumsticks, potato wedges, and risotto balls. You top it off with a hotdog (foot-long) but don't eat the roll, and fruit kabobs. Funerals make you hungry. Besides, you're making up for past lives when you starved to death.

When you were Van Gogh, for example, your steady lack of funds led you to a steady diet of absinthe, pipe tobacco, and overwork. You tended to spend your money on drawing materials and models rather than on practical things like bread, clothes, and housing. So you savor your feast this evening.

You chew your food slowly in your new life, liking the taste but knowing you won't stay away from New Orleans for long. One night when that sugared moon is big and full of itself again, you'll come back for a little haunting.

You'll scare that Pabst Blue Ribbon-drinking, beef-jerky–eating Ray and his abusive business-minded bones to death. Maybe with your good arm you'll whack him with a skillet and cut him into thin strips. Maybe you'll shoot him. And whack him with the skillet again. Imagine his surprise when he sees you standing in his kitchen in all your decorative, audacious glory. And if you leave evidence behind afterward, it won't matter because you're already dead. Missing. Unaccounted for. Omitted. Gone. Absent. Dismissed. Cut off. Trod on.

A youngish waiter approaches your table. His voice sounds surprisingly high-pitched and feminine, or maybe it's feminine and high-pitched, and it's not nice to say, but you'll say it because you're not a nice person—he looks like three-hundred-and-fifty-pounds of eunuch.

"How ya doing, Suga? You finished with your plates?"

"Touch my food and die," you bark.

He backs up. "Sorry, Suga...."

You laugh and his sponge-cake face relaxes back into itself.

"Funerals make me hungry."

"You were at a funeral?" he asks.

"Yeah."

"Sorry, Suga."

You lift another greasy sausage link to your mouth, take a hefty bite, think about how casings nowadays are not made of animal intestines, but are probably mostly synthetic. Yet given mankind's great leaps forward in sausage-making, there is still no consensus as to whether similar products not packed in casings, like scrapple and meatloaf-like shit, can even be considered sausage. This makes you inexplicably morose. You realize you spend way too much time on Wiki.

"Who died?" Eunuch-boy asks.

You finish chewing your synthetically encased meat. "A friend," you say. "She was a vile, ornery bitch."

"Oh, God, I'm sorry?"

"Christ Kid, did you make the earth and everything in it?"

"What? No. I don't...."

"Kid, you're young. Don't spend so much of your time being sorry. Did your chef cook these mighty fine links in a cast-iron skillet?"

"Yes, ma'am, yes he did."

"Umm. I can always tell.... Um." You wink at him and eventually finish your meal. You wrap chicken drumsticks and leftover cherry pie in cheap paper napkins, pay your bill. Then you sit there for a while, feeling pretty useless. Stupid even. And disgustingly, ornately full. You put out your cigar and light another. You're so tired it's an effort to blink your bloodshot eyes. Your scuffed shoes hurt your size-ten feet and nobody loves your one-handed self. Well, at least you don't have syphilis or genital warts marching across your vagina. That's something. Anyway.

On your way out, you reluctantly use the restroom. You hate public restrooms. They skeeve you out. But since your stomach is roiling like a Japanese hot tub, you don't have much choice.

That night, you sleep in the red-white stillness of your Caddy. The creaking seat begs for mercy. You give it none. You allow yourself to feel all right. Sort of. Just for a little while. And in the bruised, blue jaw of morning, when that Georgia sunshine nudges you awake, kind and warm again, you're ready for your next obtuse adventure. You've had too many little deaths lately.

6

When you were twelve, he left you in a Louisiana bus station. Your bio Dad. Your own flesh and blood. It was ninety-five degrees. Chain-smoking, whore- and crack-addicted saint that he was. Just left you in the stinky bus terminal. You, wearing gloves. And loser that you were, you sat there on a bench, tears and snot running down your small black face, petrified, smearing the tears and snot on your woolen-gloved fingers. On your lips and cheeks. Not moving. Barely breathing. Not really seeing the bodies with their unfamiliar faces marching past with their screwed-up, pathetic little lives tucked away in their pathetic little bags and suitcases.

Your hair was in chunky pigtails, little dark fists of hair raised to the world, a dingy pink backpack on the bench next to you.

You finally slipped the little pink hump of a backpack over your shoulders, your left shoe untied, went over to the wall by the entrance. Standing against the wall, you realized why your biological chain-smoking, crack- and whore-addicted father bought you that ice cream cone, took you long enough to figure it out, lame ass. And all that happiness, all those pretty, pink bubbly thoughts that maybe your father liked you now, wanted you now, that maybe you weren't as ugly and fat and stupid as he always told you were, well they all just melted away. And you learned when people were extra special nice to you, it was because they were about to dump your sorry ass in a hot, sweaty bus station with dirty floors scratched to a fine dullness with all the sad stories people drug around with them from place to place while they were looking for something better to fill the holes in their lives.

For a while, you listened to the diesel sounds of things moving away from you. And despite the ice cream you ate off the sidewalk that day, your stomach growled. You learned that homeless people, homeless, family-less, hungry, clueless, snot-nosed pathetic kids who had to wear gloves to get things like beer out of cold appliances or when they ate ice cream, weren't all that especially desiring of someone's care or protection. Well, maybe the gloves were a little bit overkill. But here's what you knew about Raynaud's: Cold temperatures or strong emotions caused blood vessel spasms. This blocked blood flow to the fingers, toes, ears, and sometimes the nose.

So standing there you decided to pull the fire alarm. Watched as people inside the bus station crowded out onto the sidewalks looking for a fire. Their breath hot. Their words hot. The air around them hot with fear and expectation and interruption. Your thoughts hot and burning. Everything hot and impatient, sticky and demanding. And you, wearing gloves. You, waiting by the fire alarm. Not bothering to take your gloves off. Your hands sweating now. You didn't care you were in trouble. You just wanted one person to see you. One person to maybe care. A little bit. Even if one person caring about you in this blue, bloated, blinking, loud universe was overkill.

A cop finally comes over. White, overweight, walks like he has a stick up his ass. Crew cut on his big block of a head. "Did you pull the fire alarm?" ingenious Cop asks.

"What fire alarm?" you say.

"That's not funny. This is serious."

"It's seriously funny," you say. "Like all these people are going somewhere important anyway?"

Cop sighs. "What are you doing here? Where's your home?"

"I don't have a home anymore," you say.

"What's your name?"

"Katrina Lalande."

"Where are your parents?" he asks, like everyone should have a matching set.

"Where are your balls? Next to your dick?"

"How old are you? You shouldn't talk like that."

You wipe your nose on your sleeve. Bio Dad used that expression all the time with people. Didn't ingenious Cop know you were trying to get in trouble? "My shit-for-brains Dad left me here. I'm twelve. Thirteen next month."

"Why he'd leave you here?"

"Because he's a dumb ass."

"What's your address?"

You wanted to tell him, you did, but couldn't because words wouldn't come just then. Words hot and heavy like boulders wedged tight in your aching throat. He waits. Sighs again. Mumbles something into his radio.

"He left me here," you finally repeat. "He don't want me back." You pause. "A poem begins as a lump in the throat, a sense of wrong, a homesickness, a love sickness... Robert Frost wrote that." Poetry always calms you.

"Jesus, Mary and Joseph."

"You shouldn't talk like that, mister."

He frowns. Looks at your hands.

"What's with the gloves?"

"Raynaud's," you say.

"Raynaud's. What's that, like Tourette's or something?"

"Yeah, something like that." *Moronasaurus.* When you have an attack of Raynaud's, your fingers, toes and other parts of your body suddenly become numb and cold. Your palms and parts of your fingers turn white, then blue. Blood can't get to these parts of your body. They go blue because they're not getting enough oxygen. As the blood returns, they go pink or red. Then they may feel hot and painful. Attacks usually occur because of cold temperatures but can be triggered by stress caused by things like say, life in general. Or being unexpectedly left in a bus station when you're twelve-almost-thirteen. Whenever you reached into a refrigerator say, to get bio Dad a beer, your fingers could turn red, white, and blue. *You're a grand old flag/Though you're torn to a rag....*

Just a small change in temperature can trigger an attack. But it's not the same as frostbite. In most people with Raynaud's, the disease isn't connected to any serious medical problem. In fact, nobody knows what causes it. So you wear the gloves whenever you have to open up a cold appliance. Or eat something cold. Or get really, really stressed out. As if you weren't already enough of a freak. *You're that something patriotic that no one can understand....* Just try flipping someone off with a red-white-and-blue finger.

Next thing you knew Child Protection Services was called and you became a ward of the state. Thus began a time of running away, taking shelter in trash bins, sleeping in the streets and in abandoned buildings, electrical meter rooms in strip malls and beneath bridges. The stars really do look different when you're sleeping next to railroad tracks strewn with garbage or on the roof of a strip mall or under a bridge over a drainage canal. A bus station becomes a place to go to the bathroom, to lounge on benches, dance, blare music; a library a place to surf the Internet on free computers. And read books and wish you were somebody else. With a real life. A real family. A real house.

In addition to child endangerment charges, bio Dad got slapped with a false fire alarm charge for what you did and a fine of a thousand bucks. His public defender told the court his client was unemployed, recently diagnosed as having "severe mental illness" and was seeking social security disability assistance. He requested and was granted judicial permission for time to make the payments. But he was rid of you.

The only thing you had left in the world was inside your backpack. The only thing you'd ever put any faith in.

7

So, it's a few months after your funeral and you're back in The Big Easy, The Big Bad Mother Fucking Unconcerned. With your sunglasses and blonde wig and big, bad attitude. Your legs and your arm and your not-arm, your fractured-more-than-once bones, your round, glistening, cocoa face and frizzy short hair, your lips and hips heavy with memories of Ray's loving violence.

So you're standing in his new beat-up old place in the dark, as still as a black Madonna in a church emptied of its greasy voices. You listen and wait. You hear him pad into the kitchen, come closer, closer to the kitchen light switch, closer to where you stand. He flips the light switch on. "Shit!" he screams. He's so unoriginal.

You soak in all his beautiful, tactless horror, confusion and shock, pull it deep down in your nasty, sorry bones and with your good arm, swing the iron-cast skillet you picked up specially for the occasion. With all your might. You connect with his sorry-ass head and he sinks to the floor. All his beautiful, tactless horror, confusion and shock, well it goes down and mixes with the honky-tonk, gutbucket blues you've always carried inside. You stare at his brown, a-kilter, ptosed form a while and, uncharacteristically, as killing him is all you've thought about for months, decide not to kill him. Pathetic loser that you are.

8

Sitting in a nearly empty bar the next day, the ice in your vodka glass doing back flips, you're disappointed in yourself. Who wouldn't be? Then you realized that haunting him would be much sweeter revenge than outright killing him. You're not a nice person.

You're pretty sure he didn't tell anyone that he saw you that night, saw your one-handed ghost standing in his kitchen, and that your ghost whacked him good upside the head with a skillet. No one 'cept his skinny, little live-in girlfriend bitch, that is.

She wasn't home when you whacked him, ga-gong. You kept a low profile in the bushes and banana trees outside his place afterward, and watched her come home late from the bar where she strips.

Soon after, you saw her skinny, little thonged ass run outta Ray's place all freaky like. She was wearing high heels and a yellow sundress and totin' a banged-up avocado-green suitcase when she disappeared into the inky night. Running away from home like a child. Guess she didn't like the idea of you haunting her and old Ray. The way you figure it, you saved her life. Ray's dumb. And cruel. And his feet smell somethin' almighty. A bad, bad combination.

See, you're smarter than all the men you been with. But you're hugely co-dependent. And your financial status ain't that great. You get some dough from cleaning hotels but you tend to spend it on the wrong things. Skillets, for one. Art books. Cans and cans of strange colors of paint that you've collected over the years. Even though you haven't painted since you were a teenager and started to believe you were Van Gogh.

And due to the housing shortage, rents are through the roof. You can't be too picky about where you live. Unless you're Brangelina, you can't afford to live here. You certainly fit in though. Crime is down in all categories except assault, and you're getting pretty good at that. So for now, you're living in a shotgun shack way outta town. In the Ninth Ward. In a ghost town.

After the storm, you saw this aerial photograph of New Orleans underwater. First you felt sad looking at all the dots that were actually broken homes and burning businesses and flooded hospitals and nursing homes, thinking about the thousands of dead dogs and cats, the drowned babies, the women raped in hallways or attics or next to McDonald's in broad daylight who didn't have anyone to report it to, the patients who died when the power went and their ventilators kicked out. Nurses trying to blow air into their lungs, blow them up like balloons, desperately trying to keep them alive while their souls floated into the water-logged beyond.

You tried to leave Ray then, during the worst catastrophe on American soil, but he had his own ideas about that.

You read that according to the Louisiana Department of Health, most of those killed by Katrina were at least 60 years old and almost half were black. But Katrina didn't discriminate—she got black, white, Indian, and Hispanic; she got everybody. Know what else? Wind, rain, and flood ripped open burial vaults, taking apart nearly 1,000 corpses.

That's another reason why you didn't want no coffin burial. You saw that horror firsthand.

You thought the National Weather Service bulletin issued on Sunday, August 28, 2005, one day before Katrina hit the Gulf Coast, said it best: "Most of the area will be uninhabitable for weeks, perhaps longer. All gabled roofs will fail. The majority of industrial buildings will become non-functional. All wood-framed low-rising apartment buildings will be destroyed. All windows will blow out. Power outages will last for weeks. Water shortages will make human suffering incredible by modern standards. The vast majority of native trees will be snapped or uprooted. Few crops will remain."

The anger from that day and all those that followed sloshes around and rises up inside you. You feel like Josephine Baker without a stage, or maybe Harriet Tubman without an underground railroad. But mostly you feel like a hurricane, baby, and you don't know where you're gonna land next.

9

So you're eating your sandwich around three p.m. in an old Creole neighborhood when you hear it. "Oh damn, oh no, baby, oh damn," you say.

New Orleans is mourning again. You don't think it ever stopped after the hurricanes hit. A funeral march. Jazz punches the humid air and sticks to your skin. Pixilated strains—a staccato drive on the end of *Just a Little While to Stay Here*—smack you in the face.

You lose your appetite, put your messy dressed sandwich down and watch the procession from the café patio where you sit. About fifty people—from different ethnic backgrounds—march together with their dogs as they remember someone else's pet that's left this mean, drowned city for good.

You've pretty much had it with New Orleans. But somehow you still need her in ways you don't understand. So you go to this nearby shelter. You walk in the door and lock eyes with Buttercup, a battered-looking, fawn-colored bulldog who wears in her eyes the pain and hope of New Orleans after the storm.

She's got heavy musculature, a thickset neck and shoulders, a low-slung body. If you had to describe her as a human, she'd be a cool Harley chick. Short-faced and broad, her cheeks extend to the sides of her eyes, the skin on her skull and forehead falling in dense folds. Plus, she has an under bite that would make Frankenstein cringe.

"A bulldog's not for everybody but she's pretty friendly and gets along great with children, other dogs and pets," the young, blonde-haired girl working the reception area says. Her pigtails bob around so much while she talks you feel dizzy. "She's good for house- and apartment-living because she's not overly energetic. She won't tear up furniture or anything like a puppy would. Oh, and she snores."

You're in love. "I don't got much furniture to tear up, sweetie. What's her story?" you ask.

"Her top coat peeled away like a banana after days of swimming in pools of contaminated water," the girl says. "We treated her eyes and ears, cleaned her up and nursed her back to health. Demodex and sarcoptic mange was treated and cured. Her eyes, ears and body healed with the help of antibiotics, vitamins, supplements and medicated baths every day. She's been here a while. She's kinda the queen around here but nobody wants her, I guess because of the way she looks. Supposed to be put down tomorrow actually," the girl says, filing some paperwork while she talks. "I managed to save her a time or two from that fate but…."

Buttercup is circumspect of humans. You don't blame her. Mankind stinks.

The phone rings and the girl grabs it. "Hello? Yeah. We got a snake here. Describe it again?" She listens to the caller on the other end. "No. Sorry. Not one like that." The girl hangs up the phone. "Sounded like some bimbo dancer who needs an accessory before she dances naked across some stage in the Quarter. Know how many calls we get like that? Not someone who'd take good care of our snake."

"I'd like to adopt Buttercup," you say.

She smiles, her eyes brightening. It helps that there is no way you can be mistaken for a sex-goddess bimbo who simply needs an animal sidekick for her sultry one-woman strip show.

"God bless you. I was thinking of taking her myself if no one else did. But I already adopted five dogs and she doesn't like other dogs. You gotta brush her teeth every day. And you didn't hear it from me, but she loves back rubs and meatballs."

"We'll get along good."

"You gotta clean her face every day too, otherwise she'll get an infection."

"I'll take good care of her." A few days later, paperwork filled out, adoption approved, you and your drooling, meatball-loving companion take off in your Caddy. Buttercup sits on the front seat beside you, her head squat and searching the windless air, drool flapping from her under bite. You think she could fit a regulation-size softball in that mouth. Ohmigod she's cute. You sing loudly and off-key:

Just a little while to stay here
Just a little while to wait
Just a little while to labor
In the path that's always straight
Just a little more of troubles
In this low and sinful state
Then we'll enter heaven's portals
Sweeping through those pearly gates

She croons along. You swear you see her smile.

Driving north, the battered skyline feels like it's strung taut inside you, a highway of pain and memory from rib to rib. You turn off on a corner that's abandoned and dirty, housing an empty, flooded out restaurant that used to serve fried chicken and fried pickles and shit like that and now has a small yacht snuggled sideways against it. The gas station across the street is the same, except for the yacht. Nothing moves. Nothing releases any kind of breath. It's a ghost town.

10

Some of the shacks you walk past haven't been gutted yet. You park the Caddy where you won't worry about it, and you and Buttercup walk between two of them, the weeds knee-high, burrs sticking to your socks.

Further on, there's nothing but the square outlines of foundations, scorched banana trees, concrete steps that used to lead to front doors that used to lead to hallways that used to lead to rooms.

You almost don't notice the brown-gray watermarks riding the backs of the buildings; they run all the way to the fences surrounding them. You try not to be obsessed with it. But you can't help thinking of the hotel rooms you used to clean when you worked as a maid, the brown rings around the bathtubs that no amount of scrubbing could expunge. Thoughts of that policeman, what you did for him while you were between husbands, his pants at his white ankles, you on your knees, sucking, sucking, your worn maid's uniform pulled halfway down so your brown breasts spilled out of it, your nipples hard, the sour way he smelled from hours on the beat; the heat, the sweat, the stain of the Quarter rising from his crotch.

After your funeral, after you came back to New Orleans, you moved into this one water-stained shack where an old lady and her man used to live. You cleaned it up best you could, tossed out the mangled wheelchair and rotted diapers you found inside. The National Guard had spray painted its availability on the outside in red X's and: *2 D. 2 Dead.*

You wonder, what was her last thought as the flood waters rose around her wrinkled turkey neck and her man's wrinkled turkey neck and her cheap, thin furniture overturned, its chicken legs in the air, floating and bobbing in mocking contortions? What was the last thing she did? Did anyone care that she and her man were gone from this lamentable, miserable, pissant, pathetic, fucked-up, scotch-taped world?

No one knows you here, and besides, somehow you got an old lumpy couch/futon and a few throw pillows embroidered with pithy slogans about Grandmoms and chocolate. You got some white guy to soda blast most of the mold for cheap. Have something that needs to have paint or grime removed? Something that needs to be cleaned, stripped, de-molded, degreased, and sanitized? Well, yes, as a matter of fact you do. Turns out a hurricane came through here and soda blasting was your best option.

So after you pick the burrs off Buttercup and off your socks in your soda-blasted shack, you settle your old bones on the couch/futon. You and Buttercup eat conveniently packaged meatballs you got at a small convenience store and then watch reruns of CSI on an old, beat-up TV. The actors have hydrangea-colored complexions and they conveniently solve horrific crimes in their rainbow-colored, state-of-the-art forensic labs in mere minutes of air-time. Buttercup don't seem to mind.

It's amazing you get any channels at all. They must be broadcasting out of Baton Rouge.

After you're done watching TV, you switch the old box off. You see Buttercup staring at your lone trophy on a shelf high up on the wall. It's the only trophy you ever got and you've taken pains to bring it with you on all your journeys through hell. You even managed to hold onto it during a few brief stays in the psych ward. Guess they figured no one ever committed suicide by trophy. Except maybe a professional bowler. A professional bowler might do something like that.

"I see you lookin' at that trophy, girl," you say. Buttercup licks her lips. "You want to know how I got it, don't you."

You stare at it in all its fake-gold, scratched-and-dented glory, standing like a ghost near the top of the house, looking down on you.

"See, I knew this lady once, who was a great softball pitcher. I played the game when I was in high school. I went for a while. To high school, you know. This lady, she became a coach and ended up coaching this team who had a great pitcher. Nobody'd beaten them yet. Funny thing is, the coach used to pitch for my high school, and now she was coaching against it." Buttercup licks her lips and half snorts. You scratch her behind the ears, rub her back. She snorts again, this time in pleasure.

"Yeah, Buttercup, this *is* a good story. Well, wouldn't you know it, we beat them and they were so sore about it that that pitcher didn't even shake my hand after. See, I was the pitcher that day. I used to have two good arms, you know. I was a lefty fastball pitcher. Well, I was more of a thrower than a pitcher. They gave me that trophy. I didn't play the game for long though. I made it up until a few weeks before graduation. Then I quit. I split that scene. That might've been what they call a colossal mistake."

You gaze at the trophy you always carry to higher ground and try not to think about the girl you used to be, drowned and carried off by the world, dead and gutted from heartbreak. You think about a float you saw once in Mardi Gras with Mnemosyne, Goddess of Memory. Zeus and Mnemosyne slept together for nine consecutive nights— fucked the shit out of each other—and thereby created the nine Muses. You toss another meatball to Buttercup. You think it's her ninth. She swallows it in one gulp. Later you brush your teeth and then Buttercup's teeth. She doesn't bat an eyelash. You both sleep the sleep of the dead, flattened out in dreams, depressed like snowball wrappers on the ground, melted, red- and blue-mottled, run together over white, wrinkled paper cones. Drowned in the flavor of your choice. You understand the language of colors.

11

You're still working on getting a decent mattress. Sometimes you sleep on the lumpy couch/futon. Sometimes in an old claw-foot bathtub piled with the blankets and embroidered pillows with pithy sayings about Grandmoms and chocolate. Tonight you sleep in the tub, Buttercup curled up half on top of you and snoring.

You wake up around 3:30 a.m., the hot dry wash of porcelain stars around you, sweaty and warm with dog. Through a small, busted up window only partially covered with warped plywood, you stare at a corner of the world that people are trying to forget and feel like you're at the bottom of the ocean. Like you can go up and up and up in this place but somehow, never do.

You can't rid your brain of the images you saw during the storm. People stuck on rooftops, the bottoms of their feet burning and blistered, waiting to be rescued by helicopters that weren't off in Iraq. Lots of rescue people did their best, God bless 'em, maneuvering around houses mangled and cracked, sitting one on top of the other. Furniture and paintings in Picasso-like heaps everywhere they weren't supposed to be. Corpses bobbing in the black water and propped against mangled buildings like frozen mimes. Feces and trash in the water. Trucks planted beneath houses; refrigerators on roofs; houses missing full walls; barges picked up by great arms of wind, their bellies dropped back down in residential neighborhoods; houses plucked right off their foundations, twirled around like little ballerinas in musical boxes; people swimming for their lives.

The people who survived felt low-down, busted-out, bad-as-bad, but that year Mardi Gras went on. Springsteen came and played. The Saints even had a winning season, almost made it to the Superbowl. Bastards.

Somewhere in the distance a radio barks the deadliest catch of Spanish music, notes punching and clawing the air. In your mind you see tangled fish lines in the bayous, a fifth of nearly empty Jim Beam in Ray's ugly man hands, little red lanterns strung in rain-soaked trees the only light, and then you blacking out, and waking up with fresh bruises over the old ones and blood on your dress and finding ways not to blame Ray. And then the storm and what came after.

You stroke the stump of your left arm, think about watching TV some more but then you'd have to wake Buttercup. Besides, last time you switched on the tube, news anchor told you a bedtime story about a man who vaulted a table and ripped the wax head of Hitler right off his shoulders, at Madame Tussaud's in Berlin. That was followed by some show about rebuilding cars. The host found two little lizard skeletons in an old carburetor he took apart. It made him laugh. Must've gotten the carburetor from New Mexico or something. It made you sad. Thinking about those little lizards climbing up in there and then having no way out and dying slowly and agonizingly. No air, no food, no water. Is that where lizards go to die? Old car parts?

That night you dream you're at a dive bar on open-poetry night and can't tell if you're awake or dreaming. You take the mike in your sweating hands and introduce yourself. "She's an ugly, vile bitch, ladies and gentleman."

Ice cubes dance in their glasses and plink in agreement. Plink plink, plink plink. The air conditioner snorts. Ray walks on stage and kisses you. Ray never just kissed you. He mostly sucked your tongue and bit you. He fills your mouth. You can't breathe. You hold your breath as the room fills with muddy water and covers everyone.

You watch Ray's hard skeletal frame covered by harder muscles saunter off stage with a barely dressed tramp with big, pointy tits, during a Cat-5 hurricane no less, and leave you to drown in a world of bruises, words and mud.

You wake up in the darkness again. Outside your broken window, it starts to rain. Your stomach grumbles. You know your nonexistent landlord will never come around to fix the air conditioner.

When you finally fall back asleep, you dream about a Virgin Mary statue, the blue paint of her gown faded from years in the sun. Virgin Mary, silently guarding the levees, her hands frozen in prayer as she floats by in the water she couldn't hold back. Then you realize what you're seeing is not a statue. It never was.

Right in the thick of it all, caught in the clutches of the hurricane, you sitting waterless on a hot roof, surrounded by black river water below, waiting, waiting to be rescued, you actually saw the body of a corpse float by, a dead black baby still clutched to its white torso by folded arms and a cloth sling. Yeah, it's going to take some magic to forget that.

They were calling it suicide.

12

You don't believe anyone who says they'll never come back to New Orleans now. Police, operating out of trailers, have a four percent murder-conviction rate. Food from out of the back of trucks, on a smoking griller, you know, it's actually pretty tasty. People have come back. More will come back. It's easy to die here and come back to life.

Eighty percent of the city flooded. But nobody got flooded like the Lower Ninth. Houses were ripped right off their foundations and now north of the bridge is a big empty lot. There's a battered US flag on top of your shack, most of the dress of stars torn away, but somehow it still hangs on.

13

Fuck. Fuck. Motherfucker. Everything unattached and upside down and inside out. You reach into your pocket, pull out a half pint of gin, take a big nip. Then you think about unique ways to kill Ray. Ray likes his meat. Maybe you could do it with a frozen, ten-pound bag of sausage. Polish sausage. Has to be Polish sausage. Has anybody ever died that way?

You can't stand it, so once you make sure Buttercup is safe and cozy, curled up on a blanket, TV on, you tell her you'll be back in a little while. You don't want her to see what you have to do. And in the middle of the night, you plunk yourself down at a strip joint on Iberville between Royal and Chartres.

While a few listless white girls dance half naked on a stage, you do a Google search on deadly sausage incidents on a public computer in the back of the room. You don't come up with much, which gives you hope. It's an odd feeling.

In an attempt to boost its stalled economy, a few months after the hurricanes hit, the ravaged city of New Orleans started the nation's first free wireless Internet network owned and run by a major city. The system uses devices mounted on streetlights to cover the city. You type with one hand.

You sit in the club where ten dollars will get you crunked and it smells like wet dog ass and red and purple lights pulse and throb over skinny bitches' over-inflated tits and flat asses. You imagine how you would have painted this scene when you were Van Gogh, if Van Gogh would've been privy to such flesh-lacquered sites. You watch a blonde with a bad makeup job and acne she couldn't hide with a truckload of beige foundation grind against an aluminum pole.

Finally, Danny walks in, and right away his mean cop eyes light on you. He has a thing for black gals like yourself. You have your blonde wig and big glasses on. Also, a comfortable, aesthetically pleasing prosthetic arm/hand thing in the sleeve of your dress. You're wearing elegant black gloves over your "hands."

He pulls up a chair and sits down next to you, his eyes on the other blonde. Danny is well past securing a desk job, and an inbred ass. He's married and has seven kids. "You remind me of someone," he says, lighting a cigarette and bringing it to his bunched lips. He's sweating and smells like the trailer he's probably been working out of. And Cheez Whiz. Has a penchant for things covered in Cheez Whiz.

"Like a big-titted black bitch I knew who used to suck me off before the Hurricane. God, she was good. All you big-titted black gals is good, ain't ya?" He glances at the computer screen. "You lookin' for some sausage?" He's jittery, wiping his nose, clenching his jaw. On the Coke. Perfect.

A skinny Goth kid with black hair and piercings in all his visible orifices takes the mike for open mike night and begins to recite some of the worst poetry you've ever heard. The dancers improvise and try to "interpret" his words with the clumsy movements of their bodies. *Boys are not forever,* little Goth slobbers. One of the dancers shakes her tits and rolls her eyes back in her head, apparently feigning some kind of weird pornographic death. Clearly, she's never taken interpretive dance.

"I asked you a question, girl. You like sausage? Cause I got a big sausage in my pants." *I'm white as a ghost and Blacula wants to drink the black love in my veins,* little Goth whines. Clearly, little Goth hasn't incorporated a politically correct term for a black vampire into his act.

You don't say anything even though you feel close to puking. *I push him out in the silver rain!* little Goth shouts. The strippers prance around, apparently trying to interpret themselves as rain drops.

You take a pen and slip of paper from your beat-up purse, which doesn't contain much else except for a little cash, Valiums, a lipstick tube or two, some white face powder. You write a note on the paper, and slide it over to him. *My sepulcher of love, why don't you love me? Boys are not forever...* Little Goth, apparently, is just getting started.

The acne-stubbled blonde bounces over and puts her tits practically in the cop's face. *Love is but a fair-skinned memory and I want to lick your body slenderly,* Little Goth squeaks. You slip out the door and make your way toward your next destination.

You walk under the domed sky. You notice a city coming back to life. It's not lost on you that you can see something in the sky that most people in America never get to see... the very end of Eridanus. It belongs to a family of nine constellations called the Heavenly Waters. Figures. Like you didn't have enough damn water already.

Here's what you know about myths and constellations: next to nothing. But you remember something from school, something that bursts inside your fat skull like a firework from long ago, from a time when your world smelled like shaved colored pencils and gloppy paints and magic markers and glues and cut-down trees. Something, ironically enough, from art class.

Your teacher told you about the myth of Phaëton. About a faint looping river of stars flowing from the waters poured by Aquarius. The star Achernar glowed at the end of the river, supposedly the ninth brightest star in the sky. But it's so far south that only those who live near and along the Gulf Coast get a glimpse of it. You had to paint that river of stars once.

Phaëton was the son of the Sun god Helios and the Oceanid Clymene. He wanted the keys to his father's chariot so he could drive it across the sky and he kept begging for Helios' permission to do it until the god agreed, telling Phaëton to follow the beaten track where he saw wheel marks.

Phaëton mounted the chariot and the horses, and of course ignored his father's advice. He flew upwards into the sky, leaving the familiar track behind. Being an inexperienced driver, he couldn't control the horses, and the reins slipped from his hands. The chariot plunged so close to the Earth that lands caught fire. Some say this is how Libya became a desert, Ethiopians got dark skin, and the seas dried up. Huh.

You kept your silvery painting of that river of stars for a long, long time. It was tacked above your bed. Right above where you put your stupid head when you slept, causing you to dream about it.

When you looked at what you created, when you looked at that painting, you thought about how Zeus had watched what Phaëton was doing in growing anger. His patience finally snapped and blew, and he threw a thunderbolt straight at the chariot. Well, who wouldn't in that situation?

But Phaëton was killed outright, falling into the sacred river Eridanus. His sisters, for their foolishness in encouraging him in such an irresponsible adventure, were turned into trees along the river bank. The same river where Orion stands, with his left foot touching the water.

A faint looping river of stars. A dumb, faint looping river of pissant stars. You loved that painting. Until your drunk, deadbeat dad decided to use it as a makeshift coaster for his river of sweating beer bottles. The silver and blue paint got wet and smeared, and the paper river of stars swelled, grew, stretched, rose, and broke apart. Silver and blue—the colors of mental anguish and depression.

You can see that teacher in your mind, her mouth moving like a river, some kids sleeping through her class, their heads on their square, cold desks, missing the winding diamonds, the silky smooth scrawl of deep space, while you swam in a river flowing through the mythical northern land of Hyperborea among the northern stars.

You remember she said something like, "There aren't too many representations of the constellations in classical art that have survived. Maybe some Roman mosaics."

You think about your former husbands. How you were married four times. About how, if you stay with someone long enough, they don't see you anymore. They don't hear you. They don't touch you. You become a ghost. Even if you are shining in the sky like a constellation.

As you continue to walk toward your destination and that cop's newfound destiny, the one he was about to step into because of the note you wrote him, you think about

when you were Van Gogh, when you painted *Starry Night.*
You made that painting while you were in an asylum in 1889.
There are eleven stars in the painting. Eleven points of light.
When people look at it, they're looking at the view outside
your sanitarium room window at Saint-Rémy-de-Provence in
southern France at night, even though you painted it from
memory during the day. Irony: each day in museums across
the world, people cluster around your paintings like fixed
stars. The ones you couldn't sell while you were alive. *Starry
Night,* you know, has long been ranked the most popular
painting at New York City's Museum of Modern Art. You
hope one day to get there and visit it, like an old friend.

You look at the gauzy, diamond-like river in the sky
above you now. You want to throw yourself into that swirly
mix and just disappear for a while. But something grounds
you. Something that's stronger than the transient things
people love your for. Something that's stronger than the
stupfuckdidy things people hate you for.

You keep walking even though your feet hurt. St. Louis
Cathedral, haunting at night, is getting closer.

You know something about haunting. You're pretty
good at haunting a man in so many different ways.

Here's what you know about constellations and
mythology: next to nothing. Here's what you know about
ghosts: next to nothing. But what you know about art? That
might just save your sorry ass soul one of these days. When
you really need it to.

14

Your heels sound sharp on the flagstones in deserted Pirate's Alley. A mist from the river lies over St. Louis Cathedral. You squint to make out the cop's figure walking in gloppy circles of light from street lamps.

You wait inside St. Anthony's Gardens, behind the cathedral. A great place to do more haunting. Katrina didn't affect the Quarter as much as other parts of New Orleans. High winds uprooted two large oak trees in the garden, and thirty feet of ornamental gate was lifted out of the ground as easily as a man lifts a child to his shoulders for a better view of the world, but the marble statue of "Touchdown" Jesus only lost a forefinger and a thumb. That's the story, anyway. That Jesus shifted the direction of the storm with just his pinky.

This little island of green in the shadow of the wall of the sanctuary is a good place for Bad Mothafucka Fat Fuckin' Mean Nigga-Hatin' Cop to get the scare of his life. At least you think it is.

The dark runs like spilled ink into the quiet. In the bushes—you seem to be spending a lot of time in the bushes lately—you remove your wig and sunglasses. You put white powder on your face. Ghosts are usually white, aren't they? Why is that? *I'm white as a ghost and Blacula wants to drink the black love in my veins....*

Up walks Bad Mothafucka Fat Fuckin' Mean Nigga-Hatin' Cop looking for the blowjob you promised him on the note you wrote him at the strip joint—he's even early—just like the note instructed. The color of his uniform is the color of predictability. There's nothing fragile about it. Predictable. Certain. Anticipated. Calculable. Expected. Foreseeable. Likely. Sure-fire asshat.

Before you jump out of the darkness, you wonder what it is that makes a cynical Nigga-hating mean cop pay big-titted black women for blowjobs in the dirty bathrooms of seedy hotels, or the back of his cruiser, while his wife and kids sleep alone in a crime-infested, hurricane-wracked city. Was it the job, the rent, the sexless marriage—*boys don't last forever/ lick my body slenderly*—the price of gas, the booze, the boredom, the Saints losing and then almost winning it all? You're always so morose these days. But you smile as you remember Bad Mothafucka Fat Fuckin' Mean Nigga-Hatin' Cop Danny attending your funeral. For the strippers, no doubt.

You guess when you sucked his cock for money, he felt compelled, in the heat of the moment, to reveal intimate things about himself; you guess he thought you'd care how his wife didn't appreciate his big, proud prick, how he had a heart condition, how he liked to spurt his streams of pearly cum on fat, black titties. Bad Mothafucka Fat Fuckin' Mean Nigga-Hatin' Cop Danny isn't a nice person. The Coke, the booze, the body odor and faint cologne of Cheez Whiz, and the whores don't add to his charm.

You step from the shadows, minus your glasses and blonde wig, and stand in front of him. "I came back for your big cock, Danny. Recognize me now?" He looks up. The cigarette dangling from his lips drops to the ground unlit.

It doesn't take him long, even with the white, white makeup coating your round ghostlike face. "Fuck… Katrina… Oh God. But you're dead…." The life washes out of his face like furniture out a front door in a Cat 5 flood. He has a look in his eyes like he's been forced to listen to K Fed or Paris Hilton CDs for three days straight. You start to feel alright.

"I came back just to suck your big, proud cock, Danny. Are you ready to join me in Hell?"

"Sweet Jesus!" He clutches his chest. Starts to gasp. Something about his face reminds you of a flapping fish caught and thoughtlessly dropped on the shore below the bleeding red lights of little tree lanterns swaying in the wind. You really start to feel better about everything.

He falls down, face first, in the grass.

"I lied, Cop Danny. I really came back for the pulled pork po'boys. They're much more impressive than your cock."

You leave him there in the cathedral garden with his sins, flatulence and elevated triglycerides. And damn, if you don't say so, your wig back on your head now and crooked, white makeup on your face running and melting in the heat, your size-ten feet clicking along the flagstones in your glittering garnet heels, "Over in the Gloryland" by Glen Andrews and The Lazy Six crawling on its knees in the night air after you, you look pretty good. Those heels could dissect a man's colon. Still, you don't want to *kill* him, so you find a pay phone, call for help, tell them there's a cop lying in St. Anthony's Gardens, hang up quickly and get on your way. *The good you do today will be forgotten tomorrow. You always say do good anyway. Do good anyway.*

15

You sit on the roof of your shack later that night, the Mississippi prostrate before you. You drink beer and eat beef jerky. Lights quiver on the water's surface; roofs jab up at grotesque angles like black shards of cut glass.

You think of Bad Mothafucka Fat Fuckin' Mean Nigga-Hatin' Cop Danny lying in the massive shadow of the spot-lit statue of "Touchdown" Jesus, his two arms raised against the sanctuary wall. You don't feel one tiny little bit of remorse for haunting his bad ass. Bad Mothafucka Fat Fuckin' Mean Nigga-Hatin' Cop Danny joins the brick walkways, the spurting fountains, the noteworthy architecture, and is just one more incomplete, sad, jettisoned story in the heart of this waterlogged city.

You feel the loneliness around you. The shrugged bowl of dark sky above you is lonely. The ruined shacks are lonely. The cigarette butts and used condoms in the bushes are lonely. The soiled Kotex pads caught on the iron fangs of a nearby fence are lonely.

Full. Empty. Full. Empty. The roof you sit on is lonely. The shadows in the few remaining trees that weren't torn out and shredded by Katrina and Rita are lonely. The punks down the block are lonely. The punks' slutty girlfriends down the block are lonely. You're lonely and your loneliness is lonely.

You pretend you're in a lonely home watching the weather through tall, lonely windows as it breaks over a garden with lonely Bad Mothafucka Fat Fuckin' Mean Nigga-Hatin' Cop in it. You think about how foul-mouthed, ill-mannered, lonely college brats were caught with their pants down, peeing through the storm-rearranged fence on St. Anthony's Garden. They probably didn't even notice that the part of the lonely fence they thought they were pissing on wasn't there. Neat magic trick, doofuses.

You climb down from the roof and go back inside your shack. Buttercup wags her tail in greeting. You give her water and then a little Jägermeister. She likes that. You clean her face and her eyes, like you're supposed to and all, brush her teeth. You hug Buttercup tight and rub her back some more. Tomorrow's your day off from being a hotel maid, and you'll do another good deed. You'll be back at the soup kitchen.

16

You're wearing tennis shoes, black shorts, and a T-shirt that reads "Jesus wants you to work in a soup kitchen." You are wearing your fake functional arm/hand thing. The scarred burn marks on what remains of your one arm are visible. You don't care that you get stares. You're used to it.

It is easily 95 degrees. The A/C hasn't worked for days. The stink of Lysol and bleach and body odor is in the wet air.

Sweat dribbles down your back as you glance up at the plate count. You've done 52 plates today. Or 75. *You lost count. Serving the homeless, poor, and transients, serving them with one arm. Serving the homeless and indigent. Serving the homeless, transients, and street people. Serving the homeless but only on Mondays. Serving mostly men. And low income. And people on Food Stamps who can't get by.*

You are staring at a blob of soon-to-be-expired potato salad when you have an epiphany and wonder, if you see the people you love in heaven, does that mean you'll also see the idiots you can't stand? You've never envisioned heaven as anything other than filled with people you know and care about and can tolerate. But what if the jerks and idiots go there too? What then? I mean, it's heaven… you all gotta get along, right?

Your whole view of heaven has just been ransacked and shattered by a random, roaming thought while you were staring at institutional-grade potato salad that is dying. Where do the idiots and assholes go after they die? I mean, if they aren't bad enough to go to hell, but they're still idiots and assholes, do they take up space in heaven? This really bothers you. And then you think, if you lived before as Van Gogh and other people, why didn't you ever go to heaven? Does that make you an intolerable idiot or asshole who hasn't learned in her many lifetimes how to get into heaven? Did you just have an idle metaphysical speculation?

You decide your sugar level must be low. You decide it's the heat. You stop staring at the potato salad. Look at the dough-faced customers sitting at the tables. Their faces and hands take in the world, knuckle-knead it and squish it around, but don't really get it. It's nearly two-thirty p.m. Two of the other volunteers have been talking about the Saints team for forty-five minutes. Then they switch to talking about hamsters and how hamsters can do it like seventy-five times a day and they do it face-to-face but one of the drawbacks, the way they see it, is if you're a hamster, you're also a cannibal. You want to stuff their pinheads in a vat of Grade Z beef just so they'll shut up for a while. Yap, yap, yap, yap, yap. Everywhere you go you can't get no damn quiet. People are always talking about stupid, meaningless shit.

The skinniest white woman you've ever seen, clad in a short skirt and a midriff-baring T-shirt, comes up to the counter. She has black lipstick on. Her dyed white-blonde hair is razor short. Every visible orifice on her body seems to be pierced. Don't think about how you feel like a cafeteria lunch lady. Don't think about how uninspired you are. Don't think about how you would paint her, her hollow, almost gold eyes, her black lips, the strange bowl shape of her head, the odd angle and juxtaposition of her bones clearly visible beneath her skin. You'd paint her as a zombie with a lemon-yellow burst of apocalyptic New Orleans horizon behind her. But don't think about it too much.

"Do you have anything with just meat in it?" she asks.

"We got what you see, sweetie. Tuna casserole. Shepherd's pie. String beans and sweet potato pie."

"But I'm on a strict protein diet!" she wails.

"Hmmmm. I'm guessing you could probably eat the Shepherd's pie and be OK," you say, eyeing her threadlike frame and trying not to notice the track marks on her arms. She isn't someone who needs the exclusive, affordable supermarket version of Marie Osmond's belly-busting low-glycemic plan.

"Are you asking me to pick out all the meat myself?" She has an incredulous look on her pin-cushion face.

You smile though you want to stuff her head in the microwave and maybe watch it explode like one of those sugary yellow marshmallow chicks that people buy every Easter. "We also got some soon-to-be-expired potato salad, some bread, some peanut butter and jelly, butter or margarine, and a few squirt bottles of ketchup and hot sauce. So, will you be having the Shepherd's pie?"

"Fat and carbs are from the devil!" she shrieks. Then she asks, "What happened to your hand?"

"I cut it off and ate it during the hurricane to survive. Now, what will it be?"

She's dumbfounded. But only for a moment. Like cutting off your own hand during a Cat-5 and eating it to survive is just one more normal thing in this city. "Uh, um, I guess I'll have the Shepherd's pie. With some extra hot sauce."

You are staring at the glop of food on the plate you hand her when you get a vision you can't ignore. This hasn't happened for, say, maybe three decades. First the epiphany and now a vision. In one day. You might say you had a bit of a dry spell in your creativity. "Enjoy it," you gush, trying not to stare at her filthy fingernails, trying not to imagine those filthy fingernails picking hunks of Grade Z meat outta the Shepherd's pie.

Right then and there, you remove your apron and latex glove. What these people need is art. What's missing from their lives isn't a perfect balance of protein, carbs and fat, or antibacterial hand gel or pedicures or steady, dulling employment or steak knives or in-ground pools or iPods or iPhones. *It's art.*

You get a picture in your head and you can't ignore it. Everything's an echo, a distortion, an imperfection. Something someone else has seen before you and you are just seeing now.

You gotta plug up the hole through which the meaning is escaping. Fast. You gotta help these people who are putting so much hot sauce and salad dressing on their entrees that everything begins to look like soup. Stop the meaning from dribbling out over their chapped lips, spilling down their chins onto the floors, being stepped on by the scuffed soles of their shoes, glopping out the windows, slinking into the streets to the get lost beneath the spinning tires of cars, or in the leaves of trees or the bloodshot eye of sky above the city. The meaning leaking from hot sauce and ketchup bottles and ends of sandwiches, burping from cheap plastic potato salad and pickle containers, from soap dispensers and napkin bins. Can't they see it all swirling away from them?

You head out the door and collide with someone. He hits you like a hurricane. A solid, strong, male someone. Somehow he ends up on the ground beneath you. He's laughing. You make the mistake of looking down into his warm brandy eyes.

17

He's white, handsome, has a killer smile, and you seem to be able to feel every hard muscle in his body flexing against yours. Dark hair. Rugged. He's one of the volunteers at the soup kitchen. You've seen him before but never had the nerve to talk to him. You surreptitiously watched him unload three hundred pounds of chicken wings into the fridge once, admiring his maleness, the lean muscles in his arms, wondering if he had a girlfriend. Or several girlfriends. Your ovaries are flipping over now and you can't help thinking what the soft hair on his thighs would feel like beneath your fingertips, or the firm line of his calves tangling with yours under the sheets.

You were thinking about the absence of meaning, the morning star, heartbreak, and puny, potato-salad individuals starving in their own lives when you hit the solid wall of his body. When you knocked him down like a full-force Cat 5 storm.

He's a little taller than you are, lean and muscular, with a five o'clock shadow on his square jaw.

"Are we just going to lay here for a while then?" he asks.

You stand up awkwardly like a visitor in an art gallery, smelling of soon-to-be-expired potato salad and tuna casserole, wearing a T-shirt with an asinine saying about Jesus on it. Yet you still hope to impress him. Dope.

He stands, brushes off his jeans. "Do you make a habit of not looking where you're going and knocking people down?" he asks.

People move in and out of the soup kitchen like awkward children who've forgotten they've grown up.

You feel like a giddy schoolgirl around him and aren't sure what to say. You feel like you might be having some sort of existential crisis of authenticity. And then the words come chugging out of you like a freight train and you can't stop them. "It's a sin to be boring in America. To be depressed. To fall in love more than once. To get married. To get divorced. To be in a long-term relationship, to leave a long-term relationship that's gone stale. It's a sin to butter your toast with animal fat, to despise football, to be less than busy every minute of the day, to think you have choices, to love carbs, to mix paisley and stripes, blue and yellow, to waste gas or ideas, to be poor and hungry, to talk about sex and depression, and to drive a big-ass, gas-guzzling vehicle."

"You forgot some. It's a sin to drink soda, try different hairstyles, think out of the box, stop being stupid, lose weight, get out of debt, single task, kiss someone in a thunderstorm, and eat preservative-loaded corndogs. And like them."

You laugh.

"Where are you going in such a hurry?" he asks.

"I gotta get some paint supplies. Art supplies. This city needs more art. Right away. All the meaning is leaking out."

"I've always thought the best art holds death at bay."

"You like Van Gogh?" you ask.

"My favorite painting of his is *Red Vineyard at Arles.*"

"That's the only painting he ever sold in his short life," you say in wonder. You stop yourself from blurting out "I sold that one for 400 francs five months before I died and was reincarnated into someone else!" or "We saw a red vineyard, all red like wine… turning yellow in the distance, running green sky with bold sun, earth after rain violet, catching setting sun in my teeth," because that would make you sound like a fucking lunatic.

You want to tell him how this sopping city needs more yellow, golden beach yellow, banana yellow, custard and canary and fresh-squeezed lemon yellow, Kraft macaroni-and-cheese yellow; about how when you were Van Gogh it gave you joy to experiment with many pigments, do an oil study of pollard willows or a cinder path or vegetable gardens where a man picked up lumpy potatoes. How surprised you were with your first efforts because they were good and you thought they'd be terrible, awful, horribly amateur. The solidness of the earth beneath your feet, how much light still remained in the darkness. Instead you say, "I'm Katrina."

"Like the hurricane."

"Yeah. Kinda."

"Matt," he says. He doesn't seem to care about your missing hand. "How many plates you do today?"

"Fifty-two," you say. "Or seventy-five. Maybe."

"I bet I beat that."

"I bet you don't, honey. But good luck."

"Nice meeting you, Katrina."

"You too, Matt."

As you walk down the street on your zealous errand, you think about how people surround themselves with tarot cards, horoscopes, chi energy, Feng Shui, séances, fortune tellers, ghost hunting and voodoo. People who eat the same things in the same places and take the same walks and think the same thoughts and wear the same kinds of clothes every day. And wonder why nothing ever changes and why they don't ever have good luck. Maybe all they needed to wake up was more yellow. Van Gogh yellow. Van Gogh, or you when you were Van Gogh, knew instinctively that yellow was one of the few colors about which there was nothing *empty*. A color that could be forgiven for its cheerfulness.

Sure, he may have sacrificed his mental health for his art. He may have been bipolar, constipated, melancholy, drank way too much absinthe, was a manic depressive who had really bad luck with the opposite sex, a fuzzy orange man who drank too much and didn't eat enough and had several stints in the asylum—and painted absolutely fucking brilliant canvases that were recognized and loved by millions only after he died, but that's beside the point. Forest for the trees, people. Forest for the trees.

18

Your vision. It involves the twisted trees behind your shotgun shack, two twisted and lithesome trees growing into the wall of a hurricane-damaged home. You are sure the trees are telling you something. You are sure the trees are an outline of Lakshmi, Hindu goddess of wealth, fortune, love and beauty. There are four branches coming out from where it had been cut once.

The two outside branches have joined together into a circle. One branch goes straight up to the top of the circle. The limbs of the tree look like four arms.

You saw in the news recently that a little girl in Bangalore was born with four arms and is revered in her village as a goddess. It's a sign. Children born with deformities are often viewed as reincarnated gods.

Lakshmi is the wife of Vishnu and is said to bring good luck, believed to protect her devotees from all kinds of misery and money-related sorrows. She is endowed with six divine qualities, and is the source of strength even to Vishnu.

You read about Vishnu once when you were homeless and sleeping in a library. You read beautiful books by the light of a stubby candle you'd dug out of the trash and dreamed of a better life. You read how Vishnu always carries four things—a white conch shell, a rotating disk, golden mace, and a lotus flower.

You think about the conch shell. For sure you don't need one to hear the ocean now—the ocean came to you this time.

Then you think about how Lakshmi has four arms and eight hands and about how you only have one hand.

The lotus in her back right hand was to show the idea that one must perform all duties in the world in accordance with dharma. That led to moksha or liberation, represented by a lotus in the back left hand. The golden coins tumbling from her front left hand show that she provides wealth and prosperity to her devotees. Her right front hand bestows blessings on the devotees.

You look at the stump on the end of your left arm and then at your good hand. It has some puckered and scarred flesh from the fire, from the time Ray chained you to that radiator and you had to cut off the other one to survive. When you became a ghost.

You think about Cornelia Adriana Vos-Stricker, or Kee. About how when you were Van Gogh you fell in love with her and she rejected you. Forget the fact that she was your cousin, the daughter of your mother's older sister and Johannes Stricker, your aunt and uncle who showed you kindness while you were struggling as an artist. Was there ever a time you weren't struggling as an artist? You were living with your family in Etten, Netherlands when you fell in love with Kee, a recent widow who was raising her eight-year-old son.

Standing in Kee's father's home one evening, you did what any young man in love with his cousin would do: you put your hand over the open flame of an oil lamp. And held it there. And kept holding it there, the smell of your burning flesh in your nostrils, in Kee's flaring, angry father's nostrils.

You kept your hand in the flame of the lamp and said, "Let me see her for as long as I can keep my hand in the flame." But Kee's father blew it out, and blew out your dreams.

Thus disarmed, you left the house with your doused lamp, not having seen Kee, feeling a little humiliated. But only a little.

You went so far as to ask her to marry you to which she said, "Never, no, never." "Never, no, never" was not something to stop *you*. To put it mildly, you didn't give up easily. You just wanted her to love you back. You think about your second husband Penny's comment at your funeral... the one he made while lying drunk on the floor of an ice cream truck... that your persistence is disgusting. It was disgusting then too, in the late 1800s.

The love affair with Kee, and her repeated rejection-rejection-rejection, triggered your first bout of mental illness. What color is humiliation?

Then there was the time you drank turpentine and ate paint in a failed suicide attempt. It didn't taste good. You touch the rough bark of the tree growing through a house. The tree that will become your mural. You think about how turpentine is a fluid obtained by the distillation of resin obtained from live trees, mainly pines. You learned a lot of things when you were a homeless pud shelving yourself in a library. Good thing you didn't light up after drinking the turpentine, as it's combustible and poses a fire hazard.

You swear that over a hundred and thirty-some years later you can still remember that taste. The taste of failure.

In 1890, less than two months before a pistol shot ended your life, you wrote to a Paris newspaper critic who had praised your work, "It is *absolutely certain* that I shall never do important things." You were 37 years old and had been painting for less than ten years and had sold next to nothing. In your last letter to your dedicated brother Theo, which they found on you, the artist, at your death, you'd written, "Well, my own work, I am risking my life for it, and my reason has half foundered because of it."

What color is rejection?

19

You work days and nights preparing the surface of the wall for your vision. The surface needs to be free of major defects and water damage. Just because this task is more of a challenge in waterlogged New Orleans doesn't mean you'll be put off.

The wall is still stained with water that was flung in every direction during nature's grand performance of 2005.

Off to your right is someone's weed-choked, storm-damaged garden and a small pond. The top of a statue, the very top of its smooth, braided head, pokes above the pond's surface; the rest of the statue's body is submerged.

You buff and prime the wall as best you can, fill holes, apply a waterproof coat that will protect the mural you're going to paint from any moisture that might seep through the wall.

You spent the past week organizing your collection of eclectic paints and feverishly sketching out your vision, superimposing a series of horizontal and vertical lines over the final sketch, breaking the composition down into small squares, so you can create a similar pattern of squares on the blank wall. Each square on the wall is directly proportional to each one on the sketch, sort of like painting by numbers. Sort of. But not really.

When creating a mural in New Orleans, sometimes there are chimneys, ledges, windows, or, in this case, trees to work around. Sometimes there are deformities that need to be compensated for by adjusting the composition or varying the paint coverage.

You kept your paints in a storage facility that, miraculously, was not damaged during Katrina.

You designed a special lift for your one-handed self that has a grappling hook and long cord to haul cans of paint up scaffolding, but Matt insists on keeping you company and helping you with everything, including the scaffolding and other mechanical things. You show him the sketch you made. "It's incredible, really, really good," he says.

"Art is a communicable disease," you say, mixing up a batch of paint called Yellow Fever and one called Goldfish with your good hand. You mix your colors in cardboard boxes and try them out on your clothes and shoe tops. Your shoes look like something on LSD.

"*Life* is communicable," he says.

"History is full of artists who suffered while producing their great works of art," you continue. "Diseased geniuses," you say, feeling the frenzy of creation welling up inside you. "Diseased geniuses. Beethoven endured deafness and bouts of depression on the way to completing his nine symphonies. Van Gogh dealt with depression his whole his life, but produced hundreds of great paintings. And Michelangelo, W.B. Yeats, and Andy Warhol may have had Asperger's syndrome."

Matt nods. He gets busy linking together scaffolding. "Researchers argue that the self-portraits painted by Albrecht Dürer reveal he had a severe squint and those painted by Henri de Toulouse-Lautrec expose his deformities," he says. "And was there ever any doubt that Edvard Münch was mentally ill?" He makes a face like the man in *The Scream* and you laugh.

Then you think about a tree you painted when you were Van Gogh. *Almond Blossoms* was a group of paintings you made during the last few years of your life, that life. *Almond Blossoms* was made to celebrate the birth of your nephew and namesake, son of your brother Theo and sister-in-law Jo. That tree is electric. It *vibrates*. Big branches of white almond blossom against a blue sky. The branches of the almond tree seem to float against the blue sky.

What did you write in one of your letters? "I am up to my ears in work for the trees are in blossom…." Probably not the best choice of words.

If you search for *Almond Blossoms* by Van Gogh on Google, hundreds of sites come up, offering posters, prints, mounted prints, framed prints, T-shirts, personalized rugs, hand-painted men's silk neckties, teacups, mugs, saucers, plates, mouse pads, iPhone and iPad mini cases and hardshells, stainless steel analogue watches, and 1000-piece puzzles.

In May of 1890, you left Saint Paul's in Saint-Rémy to see your family and brought them that painting. You died less than three months later.

Irony: when you look at that painting now, you feel calm and serene, like you are under water.

20

You think it's Thursday. You mix Robin Egg Blue. You glance at the pond. The lady statue? The smooth row of curls of her concrete hair? The top of her head and now her forehead are visible above the water. You go back to mixing the paint.

"John Updike suffered from psoriasis," you tell Matt. "In his autobiography, *Self-Consciousness*, Updike links his 'skin's embarrassing overproduction' to his creativity."

Like Raynaud's, outbreaks of psoriatic lesions can usually be traced to traumatic events in the life of the sufferer. Coping with psoriasis is as much about coping with emotions as it is about dealing with the physical side of the disease. And sometimes it is also about finding an outlet for those emotions. "I have Raynaud's," you blurt. "Not only am I missing a hand, but I have very cold fingers and toes. Well, the fingers I have left, anyway. My skin goes through three color changes—red, white, and blue—when I'm cold or stressed out."

"Does it bother you much, the Raynaud's?"

"Nah. Not so much now." You play with getting Mocha Treat right before splashing it on the wall. Then you fiddle with Cranberry Zing and start to prepare the Mint Lime.

"Jean Paul Marat, a hero of the French Revolution? A woman who disagreed with his politics stabbed him to death while he was soaking in a medicinal bath to alleviate his psoriasis. He's just soaking in the tub and this psycho comes up and stabs him. I don't know. Heroes or pussies, something eventually takes us all down."

Roasted Pepper and Burnt Pumpkin are next. Later it's Sperm Whale Blue. "Anyway, all I'm saying is that great art is often unrecognized as such until the artist becomes a corpse. Then his or her work comes into vogue." Uncategorized fact and a perfect example: During his lifetime, Herman Melville's *Moby Dick* sold only fifty copies.

21

No one forecasted the levees would fail. Hundreds of people drowned. A catastrophic failure, they called it. And now here you are, your one-handed self, daubing, smearing, smudging, anointing art and hope on the side of a wounded home where people had lived on borrowed time. People who did everything they were supposed to; people who believed in the system. In the security of the levees. Now they had nothing. Now they were dead. What color is trust? What color is storm surge?

You go to sleep exhausted every night. You are back at it again in the morning. Determined to make the government graffiti on the wall disappear: 4 D. 4 DEAD here. The goddess with four appendages. 4 X. The irony is not lost on you.

To cover death with life.

You have all your paintbrushes, paint cans, the scaffolding and ladders thanks to Matt, everything you need. And lots of water, because heat is the worst thing about creating a mural on the side of a fucked-up house with trees growing in it in New Orleans.

You are using a color you call Truck Tire to paint Bob Dylan's hair when an old woman comes by. She's tired, dirty, and smells like sauerkraut, is missing teeth, but still she looks up at you on the scaffolding. "Would you like an iced tea?" She smiles. You didn't know anyone else was here. Or that anyone had any smiles left to offer. Her eyes are so bloodshot they remind you of tomato paste. You come down off the scaffolding and glug down the tea. It's some of the best iced tea you've ever had. "Thank you," you say.

"What are you painting?" she asks, shading her eyes with her hand and the frail flap of her white bird-wing arm.

"I don't know yet. I just know I have to paint it."

"Did God tell you to paint it?" she asks. You worry that you look that psychotic. "Jesus, lady," you say.

"Oh, Jesus told you to paint it. He talks to me too."

You don't bother to correct her misassumption. Within the span of an hour, eight more people come by and offer you observations on what you are doing. Two women and their husbands say they are glad to see the government-graffiti disappearing. 4 D. 4 DEAD here, folks. A young man wants to know if he can set up shop next to you selling hand-painted T-shirts. Murals have this kind of effect. They make you see things in new ways. They touch everyone who sees them. They echo through a community.

You know when the mural is finished, you and the others will move on, doing your wash, cooking your hamburger, trying to find a way to pay for things, no longer seduced by your vision, your dreams.

You don't trick yourself into thinking you're anything special because you're creating this. You don't expect love or approval or praise or interest or even a continuous supply of free cookies and iced tea. But you know if you've dreamed it, somehow, it is.

You know that after say, fifteen to twenty years, a mural will begin to deteriorate, fade away, unless there is active interest in preserving it. Kind of like a city. Flooded. Eighty percent of it under water due to a Cat-5 hurricane and ill-engineered levees and an inhumane governmental response to human suffering and tragedy. Well, maybe in fifteen to twenty years, people affected by the hurricane will finally get their insurance checks or FEMA trailers or government assistance.

The tree weaves in and out of the boundaries of the wall of the house, going places it's not supposed to go. Somehow it is part of the city. Part of you. Part of that little girl born with four arms in Bangalore. Part of the young man selling T-shirts and the old woman who thinks Jesus talks to her. "You know what that needs?" the woman says. "A rainbow. It needs a rainbow. And, you know, a whale or something. A great, big fat whale and some dolphins."

You think about your mural, about how the moment Herman Melville jotted down the opening line, "Call me Ishmael", the story of Moby Dick began to separate itself from a bunch of other possibilities. From a bunch of other stories. Figures one of your favorite novels would be something with the word "Dick" in it.

22

Your good arm aches with your efforts but you barely notice. When you paint a mural, you use your whole body, not just your wrist. You use your feet, your toes, your knees, your spine, your kidneys, your liver, fingers, teeth, lungs, and ears.

Your vision, your painting is taking shape. You erase each red X with a chin, a curved thigh, a trombone, a rainbow, a skinny little old lady with a smile. Your mural, your vision, includes women of all races, famous and ordinary, Jesus, a goddess with four arms, Bob Dylan. You don't generally paint celebrities but you make an exception for Dylan. You paint an imaginary garden under construction, populated with different people. You see something beautiful in the middle of this cesspool of a city, you're gonna stop and look at it.

A guy who's built like a construction worker, clad in jean shorts, sandals and gray T-shirt, sporting a crew cut, walks up and stares at what you are doing. "Wow. That's gonna piss a lot of people off," he says. He's chewing on some kind of sandwich wrapped in crinkly paper. "I like it." He pauses to swallow. "Houses don't always grow on trees, do they?" A blob of mustard falls on his shirt. He looks at it distractedly, wipes it with a paper napkin. Then walks off.

In 1890, Van Gogh, or you when you were Van Gogh, painted some of his last paintings from the asylum in Saint-Rémy. By the way, after Van Gogh, or you when you were

Van Gogh, cut off his ear, he had a few stays in the local asylum. The third time, his third stay, that was the outcome of local protest. It wasn't voluntary.

Decorous adults and children of the town, worried about demented artists who cut off their own body parts, surrounded his yellow house and, jeering, climbed its walls, up to the windows, then came together and sent a petition to the Mayor of Arles saying he was a menace to society, that he drank too much, that he tried to snatch their children, that women were afraid of him, that he touched them inappropriately in public.

So on the mayor's orders, the painter was locked up nice 'n neat in the asylum and his yellow house was sealed off and many of his paintings were ruined by water and condensation because no one cared for them while he was away. Sweet. Kick 'em while they're down, tortured genius artists, because you know, he might've gone and cut somebody *else's* ear off.

You know what's weird? One-hundred-and-twenty-three years later, this is still the world we live in. Of course, psoriasis and Raynaud's are still around, but now we also have bioterrorism, West Nile virus, HIV/AIDS, new cancers, smallpox, anthrax, and the Ebola virus to contend with. Along with that show *Dancing with the Stars*. Frightening.

23

Meadow in the Garden of Saint-Paul Hospital. The canvas echoed
the subjects of those Van Gogh, or you when you were Van
Gogh, had painted when he first arrived in Arles: flowers and
the abandoned gardens that surrounded the asylum of crazies
the world had abandoned. Stunted, lumpy bushes in bold
lines of green, gold, black and tan. Fast strokes, trying to
finish something before you took the journey to your next
home with a little help from a revolver you fired, somewhat
inexpertly, into your own stomach.

In the late 1800s, revolvers could be had for 5 francs
apiece from any hardware store. Hardware merchants
frequently gave them as gifts. Makes sense; nothing says "I
care" quite like a revolver.

You think about men and guns and the German *entartete
Kunst,* a term adopted by the Nazis to describe virtually all
modern art. Degenerate. Such art was banned on the
grounds that it was un-German or Jewish Bolshevist in
nature, and those identified as degenerate artists were
subjected to sanctions. Some of Van Gogh's, or your, art was
chosen to be part of this exhibit of banned art forty seven
years *after* your death. Your self-portrait with your bandaged
ear, for example.

You sitting there like a dillweed, linen wrapped around
your blocky head, coming down from beneath that fuzzy
black hat over your severed ear, your loser-self staring back

calmly at the deaf and distorted world that had never understood you or your work. You with your high, broad forehead but relatively small chin. Hey, you only cut off *part* of your ear.

The *Entartete Kunst* exhibit, featuring over six-hundred-and-fifty paintings, sculptures, prints, and books from the collections of thirty-two German museums, opened in Munich on July 19, 1937, and remained open until November 30 before traveling to eleven other cities in Germany and Austria.

The exhibit was jumbled together on the second floor of a building formerly occupied by the Institute of Archaeology. Viewers had to climb up to the exhibit by means of a narrow staircase. The first sculpture they encountered was an oversized, theatrical portrait of Jesus, which was meant to intimidate viewers; when entering, they literally bumped into it. The dim and claustrophobic rooms were made of temporary partitions and were deliberately chaotic and overfilled. Pictures were crowded together, framed and unframed, usually hung by cord, some purposely hanging upside down.

The first three rooms were grouped by theme. The first room contained works considered demeaning of religion; the second featured works by Jewish artists in particular; the third contained works deemed insulting to the women, soldiers and farmers of Germany. You wonder, were the farmers of Germany easily offended?

The rest of the exhibit had no particular theme. Slogans were painted on the walls. For example: *Insolent mockery of the Divine under Centrist rule; An insult to German womanhood; The ideal-cretin and whore; The Jewish longing for the wilderness reveals itself—in Germany the Negro becomes the racial ideal of a degenerate art. Madness becomes method.*

You think about all those people just bumping into Jesus at the top of that narrow staircase, leaving their oily fingerprints on his oversized robes, leaving fibers from their woolen coats on his torso, darting glances at his feet, afraid to look at his face.

You stare at your mural, the emerging Jesus you're creating in his coconut-colored robe. Your Harriet Tubman with her shiny orange-peel lips. *Your* Josephine Baker with her long black lashes and skin like a shiny plum in a sunlit orchard. The old woman who gave you cookies and iced tea. Bob Dylan in his blue jeans, tangled up in blue. The young man selling T-shirts. The faces in line at the soup kitchen. Your sketch has mutated, changed to reflect the people and city around you. You can out-work anybody. You're an obsessive, muscular freight train, barreling along, painting with your good hand, strong as a locomotive climbing a mountain. A hurricane, baby.

24

You choose Chalky Green, Beige, Ranch Red, Crisp Blue, Lemon Drop. Seaweed and Beach Glass. You make Jesus's eyes Batter Bowl Green. You were Van Gogh. Goldfish and Sun God. You're Katrina now. Katrina Lalande Jones Thomas Jackson Miller. Peach Medley, Victorian Red and Lima Bean. Shy Grey and Wings of a Dove. You buy little pints of acrylic paint to tint the house paint.

You start every day at five-thirty a.m. and work seven days a week, into the night. Buttercup keeps you company. Matt keeps you company. Angles the lights for you. Gets you water. Hauls up supplies. Gets you sandwiches. Tells you stupid jokes. Kisses you a lot. He's growing into you and you stop trying to avoid it.

The Hindu goddess, the four arms, it makes you think of a painting Van Gogh, or you, did called *Pietà*, the Virgin Mary mourning over the dead Christ. Their two bodies: four arms, four legs. Based on a lithograph by Nanteuil after a painting by Eugène Delacroix. You painted it in 1889, during your confinement at the crazies' hospital in Saint-Rémy.

The Delacroix lithograph *La Pietà*, as well as some others, accidentally fell into your oils and paints and was damaged and you were really upset. Mary, behind Christ, their bodies looking nearly conjoined, splashing into oil and paint, baptized by more unholy colors than charcoal. You never forgot one of Delacroix's sayings, that he discovered painting when he had neither breath nor teeth left.

You stayed in your room at Saint-Rémy once for two whole months without going outside. You don't know why. One of the paintings you did was this dead Christ with the Mater Dolorosa. The figures of the two heads seem like one. The picture plane is divided into areas of intense sapphire blue next to citron yellow. Mary's arms reach forward expectantly rather than enfolding Jesus in grief. The figures seem to raise themselves off the canvas because you layered so much paint on them.

The figure you've created on your mural with the trees, with four arms, all one creature, brown as earth, sturdy as desire, a foreign, exotic creature, is, like your friend Gauguin, homesick, homesick, homesick with a penchant and lust for faraway, hot countries.

25

Finally, you stand back. Your creation is finished. Matt and several other strangers help you take down the scaffolding. You all sit back with cold Bud Lites and just take it in.

You look over at the lady in the pond to see if she approves. Her eyes and nose are above the water and she's staring at the mural. You know God when you see her.

Later you walk home, pop open another beer, and wonder how you'll spend your time now.

26

In the morning, you wake later than usual. You and Buttercup have breakfast and you put Buttercup on her leash, walk down the street, find Matt staring at the vision you created, which now has the words "CUNT LIPS" and "WHORE BREATH" spray-painted in very large red letters across it.

The "S" in "LIPS" drags itself across Bob Dylan's hair and Jesus' feet. The "B" in "BREATH" loops around iced tea lady and drops itself into the faces in the soup kitchen line. The "W" in whore rages across the Yellow Fever sun and gouges one of the round bark thighs of the Hindu goddess.

You feel like crying. Collapsing. Screaming. Instead, you laugh hysterically. "Any color other than red... if they'd just used any color other than red!" you keep repeating. Matt follows you and Buttercup home, says something, but you don't really hear him. It's difficult to concentrate. All you hear is, "Why don't you get some rest... I'll take care of Buttercup... figure something out." Then you fall asleep in your bathtub. For like sixteen hours. No surprise your muscles are really sore when you wake up. Dope. That's what happens when you sleep in a bathtub for too long.

You still have that ball of depression hanging low in your gut but you smell bacon and eggs. It smells good. Lifts your spirits a little. Matt cooked you breakfast. Slept on your couch. You don't have a problem with this.

You sit up in the tub, clutching one of your tattered pillows embroidered with pithy sayings about Grandmoms and chocolate. Matt is shirtless, clad in jeans and flip-flops. He is muscular, lean, strong, and you want to melt into his maleness but you have a rule never to fall in love before breakfast or too soon after your fourth husband tries to kill you during a Cat-5 hurricane, because that just screams of rebound relationship and you really like Matt.

"I fed Buttercup this morning and gave her water," he says. "Then we went and played with her old tennis ball for a while. You want some breakfast?"

You hoist yourself out of the tub, walk over and sit down stiffly at the kitchen table. "Yeah. Smells great. Thanks," you manage to say as you stuff your face with perfectly dry scrambled eggs and crisped bacon and gulp down chicory coffee. You didn't realize how hungry you were. The two of you, together intimately like this for the first time in your kitchen, somehow it feels natural. Like you've been doing it for years. "Thanks for taking care of Buttercup."

He nods his head, pours you more coffee because yours has disappeared pretty quickly. Then he stands behind you, starts kneading your shoulders, trying to help you get the kinks out. You're not sure, but that rule about never falling in love before breakfast or too soon after your fourth husband tries to kill you during a Cat-5 hurricane, well, it seems kind of stupid right now.

When you're finished eating, he leaves the room and comes back with a handful of paintbrushes. You stare stupidly at them. "What are those for?"

"You're going to go right back out there and repair your mural and then I think you should do some small paintings over some of the other houses, the other X's, you know, over the government graffiti. Maybe portraits of some local people or something."

"What's the point?" you say. "There's always gonna be dipshits who want to destroy art. Categorize it. Control it. Make people fear it. Try to impose rules on it." You, who were once Van Gogh, who even right up to the point a few weeks before he shot himself, still loved art and life, who saw rose-colored peach trees painted with a certain passion and still had to have his starry night with cypresses too, who probably more than once during four days at a stretch lived mainly on coffee, 23 cups of it, with sour, cracked bread he couldn't even pay for, who knew that the painter of the future would be a colorist such as the world had not yet seen, whose theory of art was to prescribe, not explain, you remember that above all, it's necessary that art absorb back into its bloodstream the universals of existence. Or some such shit.

Matt says, "I think what you need is a bench and a waterfall. I can help you with that."

"A real waterfall?" you ask.

"A real one. With real water. Falling."

"Don't you think this city's had enough water?"

"This will be different."

Fixing what's broken while you're dreaming. Maybe that's what art is. Doing the unexpected. The impossible. The simple. Letting it pour out of you. Lifting wet brush to canvas when you think there's nothing left. When someone tries to destroy what you've created for no other reason than they can. Is that why we first drew on caves? Because even in our hairy-assed, stoop-shouldered, dinosaur-beast-fearing, pre-evolutionary days we knew instinctively that we wanted to preserve something of ourselves, scratch ourselves into the rock, say WE WERE HERE TOO, have others remember us, a slightly magic echo down the ramparts of time? Even the way "CUNT LIPS" is written, the way "WHORE BREATH" breathes across the entire mural, is a statement, art in itself, someone's expression. If you think about it.

27

So later that day, there you are, one-handedly sweating and creating yourself in the middle of a trashed, steamy, sodden city, scrubbing the cunt lips and whore breath off Bob Dylan's truck-tire hair and Jesus' feet and the soup line people, Matt beginning to install what will become a real waterfall in the middle of your Ninth Ward artwork, the Ninth Ward that was mostly underwater after Katrina hit, and your eyes are wet now, your armpits are wet, your back is soaked, your inner thighs are sticky with sweat, and if you turn your head, you can still see the statue of the lady who is mostly underwater in a nearby pond, only now her whole round face is visible.

28

You put your hand on the tree that's part of your masterpiece, that has woven itself through a wall. *A wall.* The bark is warm, rough and tender-soft at the same time. The way the tree reaches out? Its limbs are part of the folds of Jesus' robe, part of Bob Dylan's hair, part of Harriet Tubman's arms and Josephine Baker's curvy hip and Thelonious Monk's dancing torso and the trombone faces of everyone in line at the soup kitchen and the iced tea lady who smells like sauerkraut and onions.

We are all, somehow, writing, drawing, scratching, clawing ourselves into history. All somehow obsessed. Depressed. Happy. Crazy. A cathedral from ashes. Each one of us.

"You know what Plato said once?" Matt asks, intent on his task of creating the waterfall.

"A bunch of philosophical crap?" you say, smiling and dabbing your brush into a mixture of Carnival Clown and Pink Balloon. He laughs.

"He said God placed water and air between fire and earth, made them proportional to one another so that air is to water as water is to earth, and that way he bound the world into a visible and tangible whole."

"Not in no New Orleans she didn't," you say, throwing Pink Balloon and Carnival Clown onto your vision, making it pop off your industrial canvas. "Plato was a moronic pud.

Maybe water in the firmament condensed to form stars, which allowed hurricanes to form and break levees."

"Maybe," he says. "You want to meet me in the Quarter later tonight?"

You've fixed Bob Dylan's hair but the Pink Balloon paint makes his lips a little too pink. "Are you asking me on a date?"

"Yep."

"For some rum and thunder?"

"Yep. I think we could both use some."

"Yeah," you say, outlining Bob Dylan's Pink Balloon lips in Tangerine Orange. You stand back, look it all over. The lessons you are supposed to learn aren't all in your work.

29

A few hours later, Matt is back early, knocking on your door. You open it up and he hauls a scruffy-looking teenager into your living room, his dingy blue T-shirt bunched in Matt's strong fingers.

"I got him. The tagger. The graffiti artist. He was gonna do it again. Want me to call the police?"

You stare at the boy. He looks twelve, maybe thirteen. The same age you were when you were dumped in a bus station by a father who didn't want you anymore and who didn't know what to do with you, the only thing that mattered inside your pink backpack. The thing that saved you. Your sketches. Your art. Your world on little pieces of crumpled paper in tangerine orange and aqua blues and zinc white. Your whole little paper-thin world.

"No," you say. "Give him a paintbrush."

The Quarter could wait. It'd still be there in a little while. Hell, it'd stood basically untouched through a Cat-5 hurricane.

30

His name is Troy. "Why did you do that to my mural?" you ask him.

The boy shrugs his narrow shoulders. He is too thin. "I was bored."

You tell him the way he spray-painted his letters in "CUNT LIPS" and "WHORE BREATH" shows great potential as an artist. "Art is a communicable disease," you begin. You tell the history of how Los Angeles Graffiti can be traced to the pre-aerosol days of the 1940s, explain the evolution of lettering styles and the expansion of tagging into what they call "piecing." You tell him about graffiti artist Neck Face who once caused an uproar by tagging his name and distinctive work all over New York walls, street signs, and mailboxes.

Troy shrugs his little shoulders but his eyes have come alive. "His work quickly went mainstream. He was celebrated in the New Yorker and had gallery shows in London and Los Angeles. Now, he's on billboards." You hope Troy is listening.

You tell him how painting an alley wall or the side of a house seems much less of a crime than a giant corporate billboard advertising casinos that want to take your last cent or suntan lotion on a bikini-clad, anorexic babe—talk about an invasion of public space. You tell him painting is so much more gratifying than tagging and being charged with counts of criminal mischief and making graffiti.

You tell him nobody here cares about property damage by paint because the property you're painting on is already screwed up, and the way you look at it, you're just beautifying the city.

Because you can't shut up, you tell him "graffiti" is an Italian word that means "drawing, scribbles, markings and messages." Graffiti is the plural form, the word *grafficar* being the verb it derives from, also carrying the meaning "to carve" and "to scratch." The modern definition of "graffiti" is less flattering and is defined as, "Any *unsolicited* marking of private or public property, usually considered vandalism."

You tell him it was only in August 1880, at the age of 27, that Vincent van Gogh decided to become a painter after having failed at other things, and he was largely self-educated. You explain the meaning of the term "autodidact." "How did you learn to tag?" you ask him.

"I don't know. I just did."

"Then you're an autodidact like Van Gogh."

He looks offended. "Who's Van Gogh?"

You tell him Van Gogh was one of the first artists since Delacroix to rehabilitate the role of color, restoring color with emotions. You don't tell him you *were* Van Gogh.

Troy scratches his head with his skinny arm. "How do you spell Van Go?"

"V-a-n G-o-g-h."

Troy rubs his runny nose with his fingers and wipes it on his jeans. You are always surprised, and a little indignant, when people don't know how to spell your name.

You tell Troy that an analysis of thousands of paintings from the late Pleistocene epoch suggests the graffiti artists back then were likely the same as today—teenage males. Artists would chew up a bit of red ocher, place their hand against a wall and spit over their hand.

Troy looks at his hands.

"I'll give you some paint and brushes. You don't have to do any spitting." You smile. "You draw me a picture first. Then we'll paint it together on the side of a house. I want to do a lot of the houses round here. I want to paint over all those spray-painted X's. Paint pictures of people who used to live here. Who still live here. Maybe you know some people you'd like to paint?"

Troy looks at the floor. "Aren't you going to call the police?"

"No," you say.

"I used to use sidewalk chalk on trains and walls," he says, his voice a thin whisper. But I stopped after a friend was hit by a train. Near Kentucky and North Rampart streets. I don't go near them streets now."

He shifts his feet a little. "It comes out with the rain," he says, puffs his narrow chest out. "The chalk. I used chalk instead of spray paint for a while after they handcuffed me once and I spent a night in jail. After my friend's guts were splattered all over the train tracks. We were graffiti-ing and some guys saw us and chased us. That's how my friend died. Running away from guys that weren't even cops. Cops never gave me no hard time for sidewalk chalk drawing after that."

"Do you live in the Ninth Ward?" you ask.

"Yeah. Right now I'm with a different foster family. It's okay. I ran away from my last foster father after he got arrested for having sex with a picnic table. He boffed the table in broad daylight, close to a local school. I didn't think it was right."

"Just when you think you've seen it all in New Orleans," Matt says. "You hungry, Troy?"

Troy nods.

"Let's go get some grub and talk about what you want to paint. We could use some help."

"I guess." Troy darts a glance at your face and Matt's face, then looks at his feet again.

31

Later that night, after you and Matt and Troy have had an early dinner, you're compelled, for reasons not entirely clear to you, to wrap yourself in strands of white Christmas lights and saunter around Bourbon Street, watching other people saunter around Bourbon Street, while you wait to meet Matt again.

Contrary to stereotypical belief, New Orleanians do not spend all their time on Bourbon Street. You only go there on occasion.

This time, you go wearing your cherry red dress, your heels, your blonde wig and sunglasses, your blinking Christmas lights. You're not a good ghost yet. But you ain't terrible. 4 D. 4 Dead Here. You did a little research and found out that Danny Cop, the one you haunted in St. Anthony's gardens, was resuscitated, taken to the hospital, and took a leave of absence from the force.

You feel a sense of gloating failure in your bloated corpuscles. Ah well, a mind all logic is like a knife blade. It makes the hand bleed that uses it. You know some Shakespeare. From sitting in a library on the floor, reading, when you were homeless. What you don't know is what to do with the great glots of unhappiness inside you.

Sometimes, without a man's touch, you feel yourself getting sad and twisted.

So you're sitting on the street outside the four-star Sonesta, which never closed during or after Katrina. Waiting for Matt. The Sonesta, it's popular because it offers the best of both worlds—a Bourbon Street location and class. Balconies overlook Bourbon Street. No fallen ceilings or broken siding or rampant looting here, folks. You sit on the curb looking up at it from across the street, warm beer in hand, jazz/blues/rock 'n roll/country/Celtic/Cajun beats rumbling into a tin-mussed stew around you. Open 24 hours. After 8 p.m., though, they block the streets off to traffic and the sidewalks are filled with people.

St. Ann's Street, eight blocks off Canal, marks a divide on Bourbon Street, the unofficial boundary between gay and straight sections. It's fun to watch the people here, not sure if they should go East or West.

The further you get away from the river or the farther you go along down Bourbon Street away from Canal, the fewer people will be around to hear you scream. Like the Ninth Ward. But you've never been afraid of places like that.

Maybe because wherever you go you carry that strong, stupefied person inside you who needs love, time, jazz, touch, heat, a man's smoldering brandy eyes, muscles to caress. That stupefied, sturdy person who says *don't fuck with me* and *I know how to make you feel good.*

It doesn't matter how you got here, or why you're wearing Christmas lights. Nothing ever begins smoothly, does it? Not for a curvy, vile bitch like you who's never invested in wrinkle cream or Botox. You wonder if most great artists covered up their original works. Their mistakes. Their rejections. Like the woman they found recently beneath Van Gogh's *Patch of Grass* painting.

People at a Dutch university found her using advanced x-ray techniques, and you wonder, try to remember why you, when you were Van Gogh, covered her up, an early rejected painting, with another painting in the first place.

Behind your painting, done mostly in greens and blues, is a portrait of a woman rendered in browns and reds. Her face doesn't look happy or sad. It looks devoid of meaning. Van Gogh, or you when you were Van Gogh, wasn't good with browns and reds, relatively speaking. Or so he thought. Or so you thought, when you were Van Gogh.

So hundreds of years later, the whole time people thought they were looking at a small oil study of a field that Van Gogh painted in Paris, the whole time they thought they were looking at a patch of grass, they were actually looking at a woman's face. Or a woman's face was looking at them. That's actually kind of funny. If you think about it. They used something called "synchrotron radiation induced x-ray fluorescence spectroscopy," a supposed improvement on x-ray radiography, which has been used to reveal concealed layers of other famous paintings. The new method measures chemicals in pigments. Specifically, mercury and the element antimony. That's the technology that helped to reveal the woman's face, hidden so long beneath a sunny, impressionistic swath of grass. Very precise.

Chemical analysis revealed that the mercury was an ingredient of vermilion, the red pigment used to color the woman's lips, cheeks and forehead. Your friend and roommate Paul Gauguin's favorite color. Vermilion.

Antimony was a component of Naples yellow, which was mixed with zinc white paint to highlight certain areas of the woman's face, according to a report in *Analytical Chemistry*. But not precise enough to tell us who she was in life.

Did she fall in love? Did she have children? Was she hungry? A somber peasant potato-eater, as the portrait suggests? What did she think of the strange orange-haired, orange-bearded man who painted her, his clothing stinking of sweat, farm cheese, oil paint, pipe smoke, who was given to frenetic fits of sketching and painting, who sometimes drank turpentine or methylated spirits from oil lamps? Did her rough life move too fast for her? As fast as Van Gogh's, or yours did, pencil racing across paper? Like the little wings of a hummingbird that are moving so fast they seem like they aren't really moving at all?

What was her favorite color? Could she feed her children, if she had any? Did she have a husband, a lover? Was she a prostitute? Did she believe in God? In love? In anything? Was she sick of eating potatoes?

A particle accelerator was used to reveal the woman's face, unseen by anyone since Van Gogh, or you, painted over it in 1887. You know all this because of the Internet. But you remember her. You remember painting heads, including hers, before you painted *The Potato Eaters*. How can you explain this? You can't.

In this lifetime, you've tried unsuccessfully, four times to be exact, to trick someone into loving you. You thought marriage would do it. You thought great sex would do it. For some inane reason, you thought your feminine, sensual lips, lips that betray a susceptibility to spiritual instability and emotional highs and lows, would do it, would be a plus for someone looking for a lasting relationship. Because you believed in that kind of magic. Four times before.

You thought you'd be a garden that could grow inside a man. Stupid pissant dreamer that you are. A distinctive green garden. The color of absinthe. Which happens to be a poison. An alcoholic beverage known for its distinctive green hue. Other artists followed Van Gogh's habits, some mixing absinthe into their favorite cocktails, looking for a little inspiration. Most didn't know, like you know, that inspiration is overrated. That believing in magic, well, you might as well keep on believing in the Tooth Fairy, shit-for-brains.

One thing Van Gogh, or you when you were Van Gogh, captured perfectly was that gardens, and grass, are never frozen in time. They grow and billow and burst and fade and flower again. But it took you a long time to learn this. In fact, you think, when you went out into that field with the idea of shooting yourself, that wheat field with its starry, starry skies, that's why you chose it. Because it would never freeze. It would always grow and billow and burst and fade again and flower again. It was the perfect place to lay a hand on yourself and your dreams at the same time. Never frozen. The red of your blood running out onto the living, eternal gold-brown of the wheat grass. Creating the ultimate painting, the final painting to sum total your queer life. Done. Finished. Sealed. Cut off. But never frozen. All suggestion, seduction, breath. Seducing, like the texture of paper, the smell of paint and summer wheat, the draw of throbbing stars.

32

Caught up in an obsession with the stormy mystique of Van Gogh's, or your life as it was then, researchers, psychiatrists, and neurotherapists often overemphasize your mental illnesses, particularly in *Crows in the Wheatfield,* attributing your art to the beautiful and crazed mind of a "mad genius." But you knew what you were doing. You were at peace with it. A big part of art is intention, isn't it?

33

You didn't die right away. Your brother Theo came to be at your side and was with you when you died two days later. A quiet funeral was held in Auvers-sur-Oise with Theo, your friend Dr. Gachet, and a few friends from Paris paying their respects. The church service, however, was canceled because you had committed suicide.

In a letter to the art critic G.-Albert Aurier, someone noted that Van Gogh's, or your, recent canvases were displayed on the wall above his, or your, coffin and that the coffin itself was covered with yellow dahlias and sunflowers. Yellow, yellow, yellow. Everywhere. This, he observed, was an appropriate tribute, writing, "It was his favorite color, if you remember, symbol of the light that he dreamed of finding in hearts as in artworks."

Van Gogh's paints, or your paints, and easel were placed on the floor in front of the coffin. Dr. Gachet offered a few words, reminding the mourners that Van Gogh gave his whole being to art and humanity and observing, "It is the art that he cherished above all else that will ensure he lives on."

You were good at sitting against the warm bark of an old, massive tree, good at staring at things for hours, at drawing and painting. Industrious. Driven. Good at neglecting relationships for your art. Good at neglecting to have food around to eat because of your art. You wanted to sell your works, you wanted the world to see them, but during that life, only a few ever did. You painted anyway. You gave your visions to the world anyway. In a flood of creation. Anyway.

There is a time when a face no longer calls forth history. The woman beneath the grass. They recreated her by combining science and art to engineer a new method of visualizing hidden paintings, using high-intensity x-rays and an intimate knowledge of old pigments. Old pigments.

They used high-intensity x-rays from a particle accelerator in Hamburg, Germany, to compile a two-dimensional map of the metallic atoms on the painting beneath *Patch of Grass,* knowing that mercury atoms were part of a red pigment and the antimony atoms were part of a yellow pigment. They were able to chart those colors in the underlying image.

They visualized, in great detail, the nose, the eyes, according to the chemical composition. Scanning a roughly seven-inch square of the larger portrait took two full days.

Why, I ask myself, shouldn't the shining dots of the sky be as accessible as the black dots on the map of France? Just as we take the train to get to Tarascon or Rouen, we take death to reach a star... So to me it seems possible that cholera, gravel, tuberculosis and cancer are the celestial means of locomotion, just as steamboats, buses, railways are the terrestrial means. To die quietly of old age would be to go there on foot.

You wrote that in a letter to your beloved brother Theo, and many, many years later someone went through all your personal and private letters and numbered them all and published them. They gave that one number "506."

When you were Van Gogh, you supposedly borrowed a revolver from a friend, went out in the fields you loved to paint so much, and fired it in the general area of your stomach. "I shot myself," you told those who came to help you as you stumbled back from the fields. "I only hope I haven't botched it." You told people you shot yourself in case they didn't know, in case they thought it was merely paint blooming across your chest and not your crimson blood. Your life in vermilion strokes splashed across your sternum. You couldn't even get that right.

But why did you shoot yourself *in the stomach?* There's something not quite right about that. A week before you did it, Dr. Gachet had declared you cured.

You think about a dim, swirling memory of how you confronted Dr. Gachet in his home, your so-called friend and psychiatrist, the one you thought was sicker than you, shortly before you died. You aimed a gun at him while his daughter, who was almost twenty and a model for you and whom you fell in love with because of your disgusting persistence, and his younger son Paul looked on, frozen in fear and shock. You didn't shoot Dr. Gachet but somehow he'd failed you. Maybe he thought you were a threat. Maybe he thought you wanted to marry his daughter Marguerite and he couldn't have one of his mental patients for a son-in-law.

Maybe all this time the world has got it wrong, maybe you've got it wrong. Maybe you didn't shoot yourself in that summer wheat field. Maybe Dr. Gachet's son Paul, shaking and scared you'd come back later to marry his sister and kill his father, to finish the job, followed you into that field with the revolver two days later and when you turned around and saw him, paintbrush dripping and raised in the air, he aimed the gun at you, closed his eyes, and fired it into your lameass stomach.

And because of some unfathomable noble desire to protect the lovely Marguerite and her family from scandal, you took credit. I mean really, who shoots themselves in the stomach?

Eyewitness accounts say that after the shooting, after you lingered and died, Dr. Gachet and his son Paul came to your burial and then to the house to take away as many of your paintings as possible. Dr. Gachet lifting them off the walls and handing them to his son.

At least Dr. Gachet made a sizable gift of your work to the Louvre Museum, which sort of helped make Van Gogh, or you, known to the world.

Shortly before Van Gogh died, or you died, you made three paintings of Marguerite in romantic situations. As a bride in a wedding garden, playing the piano in a pink gown, and walking down the aisle with you in a cathedral of trees.

You did have a habit of falling for the nearest female, even if she was related to you.

Gachet was friends with and also treated Pissarro, Renoir, Manet and Cezanne. This was before Prozac and Wellbutrin cocktails. Before copays and computers and paperwork and instant coffee. He had one of the largest impressionist art collections in Europe before he died in 1909. He fancied himself an artist and engraver. His most famous work, ironically, is a sketch of Van Gogh, or you, on your death bed.

So who's to say?

34

As you sit on a curb on Bourbon Street, you think about how x-ray technicians performing a checkup on a 16th-century Italian painting depicting the preparation of Jesus's body following crucifixion were surprised to discover the image of a Renaissance man hidden underneath. A Renaissance man hidden beneath Jesus. Behind Jesus.

The Washington County Museum of Fine Arts, which owns the painting, asked Washington County Hospital to x-ray the artwork so they could determine its condition.

The x-rays showed a detailed image of a man dressed in late Renaissance clothing with his hands clasped at his waist.

Beneath *The Italian Woman,* which Van Gogh, or you when you were Van Gogh, painted in December 1887, hidden beneath the voluminous folds of her dress, beneath thick layers of paint, there's an image of the infant Moses floating in a reed boat and being rescued by Pharaoh's daughter.

Thinking about the woman beneath the grass, about the Renaissance man beneath Jesus, hands clasped at his waist, about baby Moses in the folds of the Italian woman's dress, rocking hidden in a sea of dark carrot-marigold and cranberry crimson, beneath the wilted flowers latticed in the Italian woman's crossed hands, rocking between her thighs, your body hums and rocks like a rising throat of water on a skinny canal as you slurp a cold Bud Lite and sit on a curb in the

Quarter, thinking about when you were Van Gogh, trying not to feel lonely, trying not to think of all the things you cover up so well.

"Hi Katrina."

Matt stands beside you. He seems to have materialized out of the darkness. Magic and showmanship. Psychology and illusion. Art and art making. He has a look in his eyes. Is he really there? You've spent so much time with him, and when you're not with him you spend so much time thinking about him, dreaming about him, wondering about him, you're not sure if he's real right now.

Something moves in you, galoshes around. He's a place that's impossible to enter, impossible to leave. Sweat glistens on his skin; you want to fill him with yourself.

One of your Christmas lights is fritzing on and off. "I'd like to slam the Urban League upside the head for calling me their 'new neighbor,'" you say. You have a familiar taste in your mouth when you think of FEMA and other charitable organizations that took money intended to help people after Katrina. It's called hot-sauce-and-half-digested-chicken-and-beer puke. People are homeless and the FEMA contractor companies are rich. You're homeless. You can't really call a soda-blasted rundown shotgun shack where a man and his wife, a semi-invalid old lady who wore Depends, died any kind of home, now can you? 2 D. 2 DEAD. 1 homeless.

He smiles. You know you're gonna get in trouble. Big trouble. Ghosts can do that, can't they?

35

"You look like you're falling apart, Katrina," Matt says. "A man could drown in that smile."

You watch the light you are wearing fritz on and off and you don't think you will forget that on Wednesday, August 31, 2005, with thousands feared drowned in America's deadliest natural disaster in a century, New Orleans' leaders gave up the streets to floodwaters and began turning out the lights on the weather-whipped city. You shake the flickering white light above your breast. It makes a sound like an insect buzzing against the bright filament of a light bulb. It damn well better not go out.

You won't forget that looting spiraled so out-of-control that Mayor Nagin ordered almost the whole police force to forget about their search-and-rescue efforts and go after the thieves who turned, not surprisingly, more and more hostile. Nagin also called for an all-out evacuation of the city's remaining residents. Asked how many people died, he said: "Minimum, hundreds. Most likely, thousands." With most of the city under water, Army engineers had a time of it trying to plug New Orleans' breached levees with huge sandbags and concrete barriers. Authorities drew up plans to clear out the tens of thousands of remaining people while they mostly abandoned the city.

An exodus from the Superdome began as the first of nearly 25,000 refugees were transported in a smear of buses to the Astrodome in Houston, three-hundred-and-fifty miles away. Tempers flared. Police say people fatally shot relatives in the head over bags of ice. Over friggin' ice.

President Bush flew over New Orleans and parts of Mississippi's coastline in Air Force One. Turning to his aides, he said: "It's totally wiped out.... It's devastating, it's got to be doubly devastating on the ground." Later, in a televised address from the White House, he said: "We're dealing with one of the worst national disasters in our nation's history." Thanks for pointing that out, Bushbot.

The federal government dispatched helicopters, warships, elite SEAL water-rescue teams, aimed at plucking residents from rooftops in the last of the "golden 72 hours" rescuers said was crucial to saving lives. Fires burned from broken natural-gas mains. Looters used garbage cans and inflatable mattresses to float away with food, clothing, guns, TV sets. Imagine. Some chump on an inflatable mattress floating around in the stink clutching a wide-screen TV.

Matt sucks on a Bud Lite, hands you a fresh, cold one, watches your lips. "Would Van Gogh be considered a vandal if he'd written on walls?" you ask.

"Maybe," he says. "What if Van Gogh were alive today and had decided to paint *Starry Night* or *Almond Blossom Tree* on a concrete highway divider? Would we still think of him as an artist or a vandal?"

He gives your body a slow regard and you can't say you don't like it. You're not surprised to be going off to a hotel room with him. Your place ain't exactly conducive to romance or seduction. And the first time you're going to be with him, well, you want it to be special.

After Katrina, police said their first priority remained saving lives so they mostly just stood by and watched the looting. Some of them did the looting themselves, kept the goods in hotel rooms to fence them later. After Katrina, you wonder if this hotel room ever held things like OTC medicines, boxes of cereal, bottled water, diapers, baby formula, tampons and maxi pads, things people desperately needed, being horded by police.

You undress slowly, hesitating when it comes to your scarred, unnatural arm, and a modular system with interchangeable parts. It's designed for rapid assembly and is light and, you think, cosmetically appealing. It requires minimal harnessing. "This gonna bother you?" you ask, carefully placing the arm on a dresser. What can you say? Even when you had two good hands, your brain was always more sophisticated than your body. Most of the time.

You joked once to someone about getting a breast reduction. He said, "Why would you wanna do that? Those are your best feature! You want people to notice those, so they don't notice the other parts!" That's the kind of body you have. People have volunteered to tell you this without provocation. They just offered it up to you, you know, in case your own vision was idiotically marred and you got the stupid idea you were a supermodel or something, or that someone, anyway, would think you were pretty.

"Nah." A grin lights his eyes. "I think you're really beautiful, Katrina."

"I bet you say that to all the one-armed painters in the city."

"You know, you don't have to wear that. I like you the way you are."

In a bed that is much more comfortable than your lumpy futon, the animal glimmer in your brain becomes a growl. You both get naked. You start to suck him. You like to feel a man in your mouth; you like the slightly salty taste of sperm and desire. You like it as he slowly fucks your mouth. You pull it, milk it, suck it, pull it, milk it, suck it, spread your legs wide—the underlying woman—you want him inside you, all the way inside to the places no one's ever been He pulls the wet crotch of your panties aside, plunges his fingers in.

Suddenly it's summer again, the end of August, and you're twisted up knowing that for the first time, you're missing someone who's not here anymore, and you've never let yourself miss anybody before. Missing someone and something that could've been. Try not to think about your neighbor. Try not to think about how he died.

Right now, you are nothing, nobody. You need nothing, nobody, except for Matt's cock inside you. Right now he takes his fingers out and starts fucking you with his glorious cock. You suck his fingers, fresh with the taste of you. He's grunting, primal. "Tell me what you need...."

"I need you to spank me, punish me, flip me over, twist my nipples, and fuck me until I cry." You take a deep breath. "Um, not that I've over-thought it, or anything. Then I need you to fuck me until I evaporate and I'm just a mist coating your body."

36

Afterward, you eat hot chicken wings and drink more beer in the hotel room that smells like sex and crotch stink, but in a good way.

You close your eyes, try not to remember a knife thudding through and severing your flesh and bone. Separating things never meant to be separated. You try not to think about your secret wishes, your old favorites, the one that is stretched out alongside you in a long, lean line of muscle right now, on a mussed bed, naked and throbbing with your essence.

"What are you thinking about?" he asks.

You don't want to say, "Fires and feces and floating corpses and dismembered body parts," so you keep your thoughts to yourself and start to play with his cock again. You put your cheek against his erection, drag your tongue up his shaft, grasp him gently with your fingers. He moans. Up. Down. Up. Down.

You want to make his balls ache with longing, feel his power surging through him. Make him explode. You taste him, then bring your lips to his mouth.

Despite what you've just done together, you're awkward, as if you've both forgotten how to kiss and suck and breathe and are reinventing it. He kisses you everywhere, even sucks your salty, earthy toes.

You nip at each other curiously, and you rub the taut skin of his chest, below his navel, his inner thighs. He touches you wherever he wants to, and you feel like you've been waiting all these years to really be touched. Bowing to a force greater than yourselves, you fold into each other's arms. You don't want to be alone in this sunken, damp world anymore.

With every touch, he's uncovering you. The woman underneath. Just another face, looking out from a patch of grass at the lame lemon-yellow world. A face covered, a face history forgot. A face with no name.

You remember that on Thursday, April 6, 2006, an international hurricane panel formed and retired the names of five of the deadliest from 2005: Dennis, Katrina, Rita, Stan and Wilma. Oh yeah, those bitches and bastards all got names. The year 2005 was the most active Atlantic hurricane season in history as well as the deadliest in the United States since 1928. It was also the first to have five names retired.

"Tell me something about you that I don't know," Matt whispers.

"I'm pretty even keeled," you say. "I'm pissed off all the time." He laughs, like this is supposed to be funny.

He props himself up on his elbows and looks at you as you get up to get dressed. He watches. Somehow, even though you've rarely felt beautiful or even pretty, he makes you feel that way with just a glance.

"Van Gogh thought there were three stages of love," you say. "The first is not to love and not to be loved. The second, to love and not to be loved in return. He was pretty good at the second stage. The third, to love and to be loved.

He thought the second stage was better than the first but the third was the best."

"Well, that's a no brainer," Matt says. He crosses his arms behind his head, his elbows in the air. Then, "That was nice, what you did for that kid today."

"I was where he was once. Of course, it doesn't mean he'll turn over a new leaf. But at least someone, one person at least, gave him a shot at it."

Before you flee the hotel room and its chipped bathtub, its rack rates and its rumpled bed and rumpled man with hands like soft, worn leather who is trying to help you recreate the city with simple tools, you kiss him.

You find it ironic that the first person you see in the street is a drink-swilling man wearing a white T-shirt that reads: Katrina gave me a blowjob I'll never forget. Two women amble down the street behind him, holding hands and wearing matching T-shirts that read: New Orleans Needs Stronger Dykes.

On the corner of Bourbon and some other less important street, a legless man in a floral shirt sells roses to lovers for five bucks a pop.

Outside a gay bar, a lone stripper clad in only a red thong and red pumps on the balcony of a club throws love beads to tourists. She throws them a little too hard as heads crane up to stare at her jiggling tits. Welcome to the largest free show on earth, folks. Magic and showmanship. Psychology and illusion. Art and art making.

Street vendors sell post-Katrina, anti-FEMA T-shirts. The God-Squad is out, preaching hell, hell, hell and damnation. The end is coming. A man walks one of those little dachshunds on a leash, the dog wearing strands of vibrant emerald and purple beads about its little neck. You wonder if God has reincarnated as the dog and is checking everyone out.

You feel like you're in an aquarium crawling with strange, colorful lighted creatures. Some dead, some alive. You know people are out there in the dark, pressing their faces to the glass, staring in at you, but you can't see them and you don't care. You realize too late that you left your strands of holiday lights in the hotel room with Matt.

Sans souci you buy French donuts slathered in powdered sugar, and beer, to share with Buttercup later. And on the way home, to keep from going batfuck insane, you buy a disgustingly green feather boa and a Spirit bag designed to help you focus on your goals and call the spirits indwelling to work for you. You decide against the ten pounds of frozen sausage.

Later, when you're snuggled up with Buttercup on the couch, powdered sugar dusting the T-shirt and shorts you like to sleep in, it's so quiet all you hear's her snoring. And a rich voice rises in your head. The one that whispers, "Kat, don't worry none about me. I know how to survive. None of this is your fault. None of it."

Part II

37

Herman Melville, the author of Moby Dick, died one year after Van Gogh died.

In Great Britain and the United States, Melville had been almost totally forgotten by all but a small group of admirers. In an article written about a year before his death, a columnist wrote that most of those who *could* remember Melville in 1890 thought he had died long before.

Why are you thinking about that stupid ass novel? Because you're surrounded by so much water.

You decide you will sail about a bit and see the watery part of the world, so you go on over to Ray's new place and wait in the shadows. Wait and watch while gliding through these latter waters this one serene and moonlit night, when all the waves roll by like scrolls of silver. Wait and watch some more. Not much happening.

When you get in a mood where you need a strong moral principle to keep yourself from methodically ripping some cocksucker's balls off, you put on your alter ego blondeness and drive your Caddy around old lady Orleans. It's like touring an art museum for free.

Flooded appliances and broken homes and more broken humans fixed forever in their ocean reveries. Foxes and lambs hidden in a pair of shoes. Smiling pilgrims and this is not Japan and En-Dings.

You are Moby Dick, the great, the elusive, the whale-ghost-monster-of-a-girl, the woman the homeless the widowed the beaten up the oil lamp on the table the methylated spirits the captain's log the lantern in the cracked and uprooted tree the woman underlying.

You stare at a busted-up old toilet sitting high in one of the oak trees next to Ray's house when you get the idea. The inspiration. Which you know is overrated but you'll take it anyway.

You smile. When you go to sea, it's best to go as a sailor. That's what the light says to you.

First thing you do is a stakeout, so you can familiarize yourself again with Ray's habits. Sad to say the pusillanimous fucker who was your fourth husband hasn't changed much since he used to drink and beat you up. You sit in the dark, in your Caddy, and eat some crap from Taco Bell while you watch his house. The toilet's still wedged in the tree, by the way.

Occasionally some stupid-ass woman who doesn't know better stays overnight at his place, but based on your unbridled observations, he doesn't have a steady bitch. Good. Makes things easier.

Ray isn't too friendly with his neighbors either, also a plus. Mostly, Ray lives now on a block of drunks who'd trip over their own dicks in the dark. Ray leaves his doors and windows unlocked too.

So you start with little things. Objects moving on their own; one of his rare appliances acting weird and malfunctioning; taking objects out of his house. You used to be a magician's assistant in the Quarter. You know a little bit about illusion. And you know something about haunting.

The magician you worked for had a magic store on Canal Street, plus a bunch of weird props in his house. He had a merry-go-round on the back of a truck that he used for birthday parties and picnics, but when Katrina hit, he lost all the magic he had in his home, his store, his truck. His frozen, cavorting painted ponies. His merry-go-round music. His magic smile. Lost all of it. Then he had a stroke.

He taught you to be a great plate-spinner. He told you you looked great in stockings and short skirts and high heels. He taught you the secret to getting a man's $10 bill with his name written on it out of an orange. Part of the trick is after a few Bud Lites and some hot New Orleans sunshine and a walk to the potties, people in the audience are pretty much cooked. Ray's cooked most of the time too. Too drunk to notice or question the magic you are performing in his house at all hours of the day and night, and quite frankly, this pisses you off.

So you choose a nice cozy place where you can hide in the back of his closet, which stinks to high heaven because of the shoes it houses. His feet smell. Real bad. Like someone took a nice big dump on a Cobb salad with blue cheese dressing and left it out in the hot New Orleans sun to bake for days. Suddenly, your burrito is less appealing. So, like a medical examiner, you have to rub wintergreen under your nose before you venture in there.

Anyway, the closet is missing a door, so you can slip out easily at night and stand over Ray, watching him in his drunken slumber, remembering how he used to beat you with those big hands of his, and call you a stupid bitch all the time.

At first, you only lower your face to his and breathe softly on his neck. You have a .38 in your purse and you always keep it on you, in the unlikely event he wakes up from his drunk and thinks to get violent with your sorry ass, pissed off ghost.

You progress to whispering things in his ear; things like *you have a small nutsack* and *you suck ass* and *dirtbag fucknut cocksucker.* You're not a nice person.

You tickle him with the disgustingly green feather boa; he twitches and moans in his sleep but doesn't wake, and during the day, when you sit in your Caddy and watch him emerge from his house, beer can in hand, bleary-eyed with the shakes, looking around, nervous and paranoid, you know you're getting to him.

At night you run around like a two-hundred-twenty-pound wraith slamming doors and knocking on the undersides of walls. But pretty soon you get bored.

You're sitting in Ray's closet one night, listening to that bitch snore, when you realize the time has come for something else.

38

You bust out some bigger magic. The Easter Bunny, Santa Claus, even the big, bad Tooth Fairy ain't got nothin' on you, baby.

You bother Ray every chance you get. When he's on the toilet, reading an old copy of Penthouse and trying to get his dick to stand up, you rattle pipes, sound your footsteps from above, whisper down pipes, take special pleasure in banging on radiators, and now you can hear him talking to himself, by now thinking he's crazy and truly haunted. Magic and showmanship. Psychology and illusion. Art and art making.

You can do it all in fishnets and heels or sweaty underpants, shorts, a T-shirt, and ratty sneakers.

Sometimes you look in his bathroom window when he's "dropping the kids off at the pool," let him meet your eyes for a micro second, and drop down outta sight on your hands and knees real quick. He mutters, "Holy Shit! Who's that? Katrina? But you's dead! You's dead! Ah, leave me alone, Katrina! Can't a man take a shit in peace?"

The coup de grace comes, not surprisingly, when he's taking another shit. By now, you've found ways to become the water in the sink, the H_2O in the bathtub, the wetness flushing and gushing in his toilet, the stream in the shower. The runnel he brushes his teeth with.

So he's sitting on the john one day, reading Hustler, and feels a decidedly hard assed-pinch. "Mothafucka!" he shouts, standing up, magazine in one hand, wiping his butt furiously and unexpectedly, his eyes wide, peering cautiously into the toilet, pulling madly to get his drawers up, running out in the street with toilet paper sticking to his tennis shoes and looking at his house like it's possessed.

A few of his neighbors come out and stare at him. Some laugh outright. Others cover their mouths and try to hide it. Clothespins are marvelous inventions.

Next day he's in the shower and feels a "slap" amidst the raining streams of water. You do stuff like that for about another week.

Then one night you stand by his bedside, looking down at him, pocketknife in your hand, and realize he just ain't worth it. It's a rotten mothafuckin' cocksuckin' world, and what would you change by killin' one more stupid-ass fucknut? One more can't-see-the-forest-for-the-trees kind of moron?

You almost feel sorry for him but stop yourself. You remember once he told you how as a kid, he got bit by a spider. On his penis. Suffered an eight-hour erection and had problems for the rest of his life with his shaft. So he claimed.

You leave the pocketknife for him to find the next morning, lying on the bed next to him like an angry lover, 'cause you know nothin' in the world will freak him out more than that. Still, you aren't going to let him go unpunished for trying to kill you and cover it up. For what he did to your neighbor. You're just kinda tired of haunting his lame ass and need a different plan. You're not going to kill him; that would be too good for him. So what then?

Before Katrina Hit

39

"Ain't gonna be no big *deal,*" Ray said when the news reporters started to warn everyone about Katrina. "Just another bitch ass storm that won't get us. You're stayin' right here with me."

Then, "lover." Ray plopped his butt down in his beat-up blue recliner and flipped up the lever, propped up his feet, clicked the remote from channel to channel. Kept clicking the damn remote. Click click click click click. "Look, damn it, I been in jail five or six times and I been married at least three or four. This fuckin' storm don't scare me none."

The TV was new. You had no idea how he got his hands on it. Like the others, you knew it wouldn't last long. When Ray got really bad on a drunk, he took a baseball bat to the TVs, shattering their plastic unblinking eyes and shouting things about his mother. You made a note that he had power in his swing, but no grace, none at all.

Maybe it was just you, but Ray's plan of being drunk on his recliner didn't seem like a real prudent way to meet impending hellfire and doom. Sitting in a recliner with his feet propped up when the official policy is: Get the hell out of NOLA *now.*

Soon the levees breached. You think it was then that you snapped; listening to that click, click, click of the remote, thinking, I ain't gonna die here with him. I ain't gonna die here with him. Click. I ain't gonna die here with him. Click click click click click!

Standing there, trying not to shake, you made a decision. You were gonna leave everything behind, everything, and just walk out that door. Whatever you didn't have out there had to be better than everything you had here.

You watched as water began rushing down the street in your neighborhood like a big, curled fist. You looked again out the front window of the living room, and could not believe what you saw. Strong winds, boards just blowing down the street. The water was in the driveway now, halfway up the tires of Ray's old Buick.

"We gotta go *now,*" you said. "Ray, the water's in the driveway!" Ray didn't look up from the TV.

"These stupid news anchor bitches. They don't know shit. We survived Betsy and Rita and that other bitch, what's her name."

"That other bitch Andrew?" you say, and head toward the front door.

"Shut up already, bitch. Fuck you. Where you goin', anyway, bitch?"

"I wanna check on some of the neighbors. Some of them are real old, Ray. They might need help."

Ray snorts. "Fuck the old fucks," he says.

You moved slowly toward the door so you wouldn't make him suspicious or jumpy. Plus, you were watching out the windows to make sure that when you dashed outside, you weren't gonna get hit in the head with no flying boards. You were done bein' Ray's punchin' bag and you weren't gonna stick around for a hurricane bitch to finish the job.

You ran next door to check on your neighbor, Louis, running in water up to your ankles. Louis was a nice man. Good-looking, too. You fell in love with him shortly after you married Ray but you were trapped in an impossible situation and couldn't do anything about it. Louis' eyes were electric and warm. He noticed your bruises but never said anything about them, just frowned.

Ray didn't like it when you visited Louis, even though there was nothing going on between the two of you.

"Lou?" you called through his screen door, which didn't latch properly and was flapping in the strong wind.

"Come in, hurry," he said.

You stepped inside and saw a small bag by the door. "I was just gonna check on you. We need to get outta here, Kat. The Mayor is finally tellin' everyone to evacuate. Get out. We'd be fools to stay. Not that I care, but where's Ray?"

"He won't leave. He doesn't want me to leave either."

Then Ray came busting through the door. "You bitch whore! What're ya doin' here? I told you, the storm ain't no big deal! Come home." He grabbed your arm painfully.

"Let her go," Lou said, low and calm, the sound of his voice like a wall of mud smacking into Ray's face. It made even Ray hesitate and he dropped your arm.

You could smell the heavy booze floatin' outta Ray's pores. He looked at you hard then at Lou. "Stinky-assed whore," he said and left.

None of you knew then that most of the city would be underwater soon, everything black as black can be, no lights, power lines down and tangled in the water and mud, houses doing the fox trot in the air and slamming into each other, a waxy moon drifting over the razed stubble of what used to be neighborhoods, toxic silt and trash and lost dreams pilin' up like great snow hill mountains. And you thought, Oh hell. This is it.

You felt all messed up, but you felt something else too. Something odd. A glimmer. Hope?

"Even if that mean dumb ass won't get outta the city, we'll leave together," Lou said.

Your life had been full of evasions and avoidances, dances in long shadows, waltzes of fear in full daylight. No more.

Lou took your arm gently. He looked into your eyes. The sound of the screen door slamming open again cut off whatever it was he was about to say.

40

You both turned to see Ray standing there, a strange light in his eyes, a Glock in his hand. You didn't even know he had a Glock.

A duffle bag hung from the curled fingers of his other hand. When someone shoves a Glock in your face, you usually do what they say.

Especially a crazy fucker like Ray. "Upstairs," Ray said, motioning with the Glock. You went up first, followed by Lou, followed by Ray. You climbed numbly to the second floor, sweat bubbling on your bodies as Ray sang a song by Annette Hanshaw. One of your favorites. Something about evil trying to get into your room.

"Let's do you first," Ray said, holding the Glock against Lou's head while he slipped a pair of handcuffs from the bag. Lou looked like he would kill Ray on the spot if Ray didn't have a Glock pressed to his head.

Ray cuffed him to a radiator in one of the bedrooms, and when you made to move toward Lou, he swung the gun back at you and laughed. Sweat poured from Lou's forehead. There was a sound like thunder. Below you, floodwater was now breaking windows, swirling over windowsills, banging into things like furniture and walls.

Ray stepped away from Lou, admiring his handy work. "Now you," he said. You moved toward the radiator and Ray shook his scraggy head. "Uh uh, baby. You ain't gonna be together." He motioned for you to head back into the hall and herded you into a bedroom across the hall. He stuck the Glock to your head and you almost wished he'd pull the trigger. Instead he pulled another set of handcuffs from the bag and handcuffed you to a radiator too.

As he was leaving, you gave him the finger with your free hand. He laughed. "See you in hell, Katrina." And then he was gone, somehow, you don't know how, out into the wide, wet world.

41

"Lou!" you yelled. "Can you hear me?"

"Yeah," he called back. "Try to stay calm, Kat."

"I don't have a cell phone. Do you?"

"No," he yelled.

"What are we going to do?" You could see out the bedroom window. The water was getting really high now. Katrina was a cavalcade, marching, screeching, getting louder by the minute. Taking whole houses off their foundations! Rain slashed through the half open window, glopped onto the soggy carpet.

This was all your fault. You could hear Lou yanking on the radiator. You yanked at your handcuffs too, a mad symphony of metal clinking against metal. You stared in dismay at the door to the hall as you saw black water, several inches of it, flow by. You saw something out of the corner of your eye, turned, caught your own reflection in a mirror. "I'm sorry Lou! I'm sorry!"

"It's not your fault, Kat. None of this is your fault."

And then you started laughing. Hysterically.

It's all my fault.

42

The water danced into your room, started to sweep things along with it. Things on the floor. Pieces of furniture. Chairs. Fishing poles. A desk flipped over. It was a struggle to breathe in the cloying heat. The wind howled and screamed. The house shook. Looking out the lone window, you saw a house collapse. You heard someone's dog wail. Deep and lonely. Frightened to death. You heard screams. Saw people swept up in the water.

Somewhere close by, a transformer blew up.

Outside, something else exploded and the noise was much closer, much louder. You smelled smoke and gas. "I don't want to die here. I won't die here," you sobbed.

Many people with Raynaud's are able to find relief by simply adjusting their lifestyle. For example:

Protect yourself from the cold and the wet.
Avoid excessive emotional stress.
Do not use vibrating, sharp tools.

You closed your eyes briefly. Opened them. Saw fire now, greedy bright orange flames licking the house next door, jumping and popping, and then you realized it wasn't the house next door that was burning but the house you were trapped in. You heard glass breaking, splintering, wood groaning and snapping.

Angry. With you.

What a doctor might do for Raynaud's:

For more severe cases that require medication, your doctor might prescribe drugs that keep your blood vessels from narrowing and help them dilate, such as nifedipine, diltiazem, or nitroglycerin. Some of these medications may have side effects that you should discuss with your doctor before taking.

A doctor might also advise non-medication treatment:

Biofeedback has been demonstrated to be safe and effective for some individuals. This is a technique designed to help a person gain control over involuntary body functions, such as skin temperature, heart rate, or blood pressure.

In rare instances, a sympathectomy may be performed. This operation cuts the nerves that may also be affecting the blood vessels to the fingers. This procedure is usually not necessary and may only work for a short period of time. But this is what a doctor did for you, queef cake.

The water was getting higher. Like a lover, swirling darkly around your knees, inching up your thighs, wet and damp and dark, without boundaries. "Lou!" you yelled. "Lou!" There was no answer now.

All you needed to do was find a way to cut off your own hand, somehow stop the bleeding, save Lou, get on the roof, get rescued, and get treated so infection didn't set in. You started to laugh again. Tried not to think of that movie you watched on cable, where Hannibal Lector whacked off his own hand after Clarice, the FBI agent, handcuffed herself to him.

Maybe God gave you Raynaud's because he knew this moment would come, and maybe, you thought, cutting your own hand off wouldn't hurt as much because the nerves had already been damaged. Plus, your wrist had been broken before. This is what you told yourself in that drowned, drenched moment.

"Did Ray break it?" you heard Lou ask but you knew it wasn't really Lou talking. "Lou! Lou!" Still no answer.

"Yeah," you said to Lou, remembering how the fake pearls at your wrist broke apart too, snapped when Ray snapped the bones in your wrist, the little white globes rolling and trotting across the floor, flashing like little sundials in the afternoon light, your wrist hanging limp, your heart in bone-shock.

Your brother gave you those when you were twelve and he was ten. You don't know where your brother is now. You haven't known for a long time. You never felt so sad. "Were you ever happy with him? Even for ten minutes?" you think you heard Lou ask.

"No, Lou, I wasn't," you sob out loud. But nobody could hear you anymore. And then like magic, although you didn't believe in that anymore, a wooden toolbox was lifted up by thick rolling palms of water and floated right in front of you, practically handed to you. It must've been behind the desk. You grabbed it, got it open.

There was some fishing stuff in it. A knife inside. A pocketknife. Pretty sharp, but it wouldn't cut through metal. You tried to cut the handcuff off. No dice. Much easier to cut off an ear.

The water was at your thick waist now. The fire was closer too, hotter. Your skin started to drip off your arm like melting plastic.

You did this before. Piece of cake. Only that time it was your ear you cut off.

"How much do you want to live?" you yelled, not sure if you were shouting for Lou or for yourself. You swallowed hard. "This is going to hurt like hell but I can survive it."

You stared at the groove on your hand where it joined your wrist. You knew about the tender gap between the bones. A sharp knife could cut through it. You flexed your wrist in preparation for what you knew you had to do.

43

You see your white angular face in the mirror again. You raise the razor to your pink ear.

You see your round, black face in the mirror and your scared eyes. You raise the pocketknife to your brown wrist.

You feel warmth running down the side of your face, down your cheeks, into your orange beard. You taste a mixture of blood and tears in your mouth. It's running down your shoulder and your arm. Connecting your ear, connecting your wrist and hand, connecting your life as Van Gogh and your life now. Somehow.

You can't help but think of a midnight miracle. A little incident that's recorded in all four gospels. In the Garden of Gethsemane, when a soldier sliced the ear off one of the high priest's servants with his sword. But Jesus answered, "No more of this!" And he touched the man's ear and healed him.

44

It's two days before Christmas in the year 1890. December 23. It's cold and dark and wet. You are somewhere in the French countryside. You hear singing wafting through the windows of your Yellow House; you hear angelic voices rising in unison, from a nearby church.

Your sadness wells up inside you. You want to cry but you can't. You don't want to hear those angelic voices anymore! Stop! Stop! This night, apparently, you chased your friend Gauguin with a razor but didn't cut him with it.

You place part of your fleshy ear, the part you just severed from your head, in a packet, wrap it in newspaper, shove a dark beret over your wounded head, and leave the Yellow House. You walk across the Place Lamartine, through the ramparts and on to 1 Rue du Bout d'Arles, which takes you less than five minutes. This area is in the north of the old town, just before the ramparts, and not far from the railway station.

A half hour before midnight, you speak to a man at the door of a brothel. You ask to see Rachel and hand over the packet. She opens it, her eyes grow wide, you say something like "take good care of this object" and she faints. Virginie Chabaud, the madame in charge, quickly appears. You flee the brothel immediately and return to your Yellow House. You are very distraught about a recent quarrel with your friend and roommate of nine weeks, Paul Gauguin, but you can't really remember anything about it just now.

A commotion develops at the brothel. A policeman, Alphonse Robert, arrives shortly afterwards. He is handed the package just before midnight. You are in need of a *big, bad-ass midnight miracle right about now.*

45

The next day, wet, bloody towels are still scattered on the stone floor of both ground-floor rooms of your Yellow House. The blood has soiled practically everything and the little stairway that leads up to your bedroom. You went to bed and fell asleep after delivering your ear to Rachel, but only after closing the shutters and placing a lighted lamp on a table near the window. Within ten minutes the whole street reserved for prostitutes was in an uproar and people gossiped about you and your ear. Your friend Gauguin came home in the morning and was pretty much immediately suspected of murder, given the bloody scene in the Yellow House, and the fact that everyone thought you were dead because you had the sheet pulled up over your unconscious ball of a head.

He shook you and woke you; you were weak and confused. You told him not to eat the fruit of the women in Martinique; they put magical charms on the fruit they sold in order to ensnare you. You're not sure, but you think you told him you loved him.

It was cold and damp in the Yellow House. You were shivering. Someone lit a fire in the fireplace of your bedroom to provide some meager warmth; there was a lot of confusion. Deep blue, purple, lavender and olive-silver confusion.

You were always kind of short on tact and diplomacy. You may have yelled at Paul. May have. Probably did.

Almost certainly. You may have yelled at the police. May have. Probably did. Almost certainly. When it came to painting, you were a romantic and Paul was a primitive. Loveable, unbearable you. You wanted a passionate engagement with whatever you painted, a person, a place, a potato, a wheat field, a potato-eater.

You liked to smear and slash tubes of pigment on the canvas. Paul shouldn't have looked down on you for that. Paul thought painters should get their orgasms from the eye. That ecstasy was visual, not sexual.

Later, with the quiet of the nearby ocean in his full, unsevered ears, Gauguin on the remote Marquesas Islands, in his last house, carved the words "House of Pleasure" on the wall.

Once he said to a friend "Don't fuck too much." He went on to write, "If we want to be really potent males in our work, we must sometimes resign ourselves to not fuck much, and for the rest be monks or soldiers, according to the needs of our temperament." His reasoning? If a man fucked too much, his painting would be all the more spermatic.

46

You really didn't feel much when you began to slice the pocketknife through the soft, brown flesh of your wrist. I mean, what's the difference, really, between an ear and a hand? You've done this before. Severed a body part. Maybe not in this lifetime, but in a previous one.

You cut quickly back and forth. The only brief pain was when you felt the nerves. You could sort of feel the nerves you had left as you cut your hand off, blood spurting out, and you guessed the fire kept you from going into shock or passing out and maybe even cauterized the wound. You were free.

Your hand plopped into the water, got wedged against the radiator. Bumped gently, back and forth, bump, bump, bump, doing some odd sort of hypnotic dance, like it was trying to shake another hand. *A handshake, I must go back to the hospital, but shall soon be out for good. Take this object and remember me. Yours, Vincent.* Or something like that.

47

While you remember that your friend Paul Gauguin did occasionally use a knife to paint, it was not his primary method of painting, and it was certainly not what he would have used to paint a face. Gauguin himself had a handsome, rugged face.

For his art, he abandoned his home in France, his religion, his job, his wife and five children. Gauguin was also attracted to men. He died of venereal disease, pretty much alone, on a remote Polynesian island with diseased coconut trees sporting hot, shriveled leaves, where the princesses went barefoot, wore ink-black dresses and fragrant flowers in their hair and behind their ripe, brown ears.

You wonder if Gauguin ever thought about your ear when he stood smoking cigarettes on the sand at the edge of the world, trying to avoid thoughts of tomorrow, of the future, of the eternal struggle against idiots.

Right now you can't hear anything except the wind, and it sounds like feet marching on cobblestones. The feet of idiots marching on cobblestones. The kind of wind that breaks things apart. Things like yellow houses and telephone poles and friendships and dreams and cars and boats and little things like, say, barges.

You are miffed that your friend Paul Gauguin went to witness a guillotine execution shortly after you severed your ear. After not sleeping for three days, your friend Paul apparently stood outside in the cold to watch this spectacle, calmly making sketches. At first, the guillotine got stuck in the wrong position, and thus stuck in the wrong position in the guy's head, and they had to fix it. It was not a clean cut. Once they finally got the guy's head off, they rinsed it in a bucket and held it up for all to see.

Gauguin lived his final years cut off from civilization, like the head, on the tiny South Pacific island of Hua Oa, an island of steamy tropical jungles and volcanoes, of black sand and pink skies and dark sensual women who bathed in the waterfalls and rivers and while doing so, pulled their skirts up over their waists to cool their naked selves.

When Gauguin died all alone in his hut, wracked with morphine addiction and the ravages of venereal disease, they found an unfinished painting on his easel: a conventional winter landscape of a charming French country village. So maybe he missed you too. Maybe. A little.

Gauguin experienced bouts of depression, even attempted to kill himself once. The vogue for his work started soon after his death. When he was near the end of his painted life, his feet and legs were so bad he had to bind them each day. He couldn't wear shoes, could barely walk, but he painted and drank and painted some more. Drank some more, painted some more… tied his feet and legs up, painted, drank, and painted.

Ain't posthumous fame a bitch?

The island's government hated him because he cursed it for not letting the natives keep their customs. The church hated him because he ridiculed it. But they still buried him in a Catholic cemetery. His body was carried by four muscular Marquesans up a tropical, shaded trail. The place where they buried him, your friend and one of the leaders of the Post-Impressionist painter movement, was a cemetery covered with long, creeping vines. The legs and feet that wouldn't walk anymore, laid there, the bones of the painter who, perhaps more than any other man, made the Marquesas Islands known to the world, laid there. You always missed him acutely after he left. You didn't mean to chase him with a razor. You really didn't. You're not even sure why you did it.

48

In case you're wondering, a sympathectomy is a surgical procedure that destroys nerves in the sympathetic nervous system. The procedure is done to increase blood flow and decrease long-term pain in certain diseases that cause narrowed blood vessels. It can also be used to decrease excessive sweating. This surgical procedure cuts or destroys the sympathetic ganglia, collections of nerve cell bodies in clusters along the thoracic or lumbar spinal cord.

Missing a hand now, a hand once afflicted with Raynaud's and once sympathectomized, if there is such a word, you pushed off into the cold water, made your way clumsily toward the hall, toward the room Lou was in, holding your throbbing, screaming stump.

You didn't see the sudden swell of water until it was too late and it knocked you under. You swallowed a bunch of it, tumbled around, lost your bearings, scraped your face against carpet and the sharp corners of floor molding.

Your lungs felt like they would burst when you hit your head against a wall. Gulp-choking on the dark Mississippi, dark, only getting darker, seeing a light, the window, swimming toward it. Instinctively you pushed both hands against a wall and the explosion of pain from your freshly severed stump felt like knives all over your body. You pushed your head up, up, up, found a tiny corner of air to breathe, finally, to suck in, damp, dirty, swirling air, and there, pinned against a wall with a picture of Jesus on it rocking and staring down at you, you, the degenerate, you, lame bones, you, who tried to turn, tried to head back for Lou, but it was no use. You couldn't fight a fat tongue of river determined on taking all your breath, licking you all over, swishing you around in its mouth. It felt like you were in a darkened theater, up on stage, tangled in the long, heavy hanging velvet drapes that opened and closed between acts.

It seemed like it took you a long time, but you finally reached the nearest window and clawed your way out, coughing and sputtering and choking. Jesus watched you the entire way.

49

Crawling out the small window, clutching hard to the roof with one hand, your back bent and your buttocks jutting out and your feet precariously placed on a crumbling ledge of painted wood, you knew Lou was dead.

Slippery with your own blood, your body just a small ache of what it used to be, you heard his voice and couldn't explain it. You knew he was dead.

The room he was in, the room beneath you, was under water. Under water. Water poured out the busted and cracked windows.

"Kat, don't worry none about me. I know how to survive."

But the brown-gray waters swallowed him anyway as you clawed your way to the roof, sat down on the hot surface and held your stump. You rocked it back and forth like a baby, back and forth, didn't even feel your stupid tears. You don't know how long you sat there, waiting to be rescued.

The whole ball of the world was crashing against your city. You were missing a hand. You cut off your own ear when you were Van Gogh. The whole world crashing, screaming against your drowned Yellow House. The whole world crashing, screaming against your city now. The whole wide, wet screaming world. What was amazing to you is *how many people couldn't hear it.*

Sitting there, you realized every man who's ever passed through your life has been your father in some manner. And you, waiting and expecting each one to dump your sorry ass in a hot, stinking bus station. You bent over and threw up, heard the meager contents of your stomach splash into the water below, knowing everybody who'd been in that water and survived was gonna need some kind of vaccination. Then you threw up again.

Hours and hours later, harnessed and being lifted to the helicopter, being rescued, the city below could've been a Polynesian island lost in a hurricane. You thought about your friend Gauguin, about how you were barefoot now because somehow you lost your shoes, about how you had no flowers pinned behind your brown ears and your dress wasn't black, it was pink, pink and grubby with your spit and vomit.

Sitting in the helicopter airlift rescue thingie, you sang. Ann Rabb's "It Wouldn't Make Me Love You More." You shouted-sang but couldn't hear your own voice over the sound of the copter's whirring blades and the wind, but you could feel the vibrations of air in your throat and it was some small comfort.

50

You waited on the roof of a partially burning house with Lou's dead and drowned body floating and chained to a radiator on the floor below you. Occasionally other people who were also stuck on roofs shouted encouragement. Some shouted swear words.

It was odd not to hear insects chirping or car motors. You heard others moaning and pounding their fists on the inside of their attics like they were trapped inside a womb, the sound like drums, the slow, far away death beat of Polynesian island drums; you looked down and saw venomous snakes sliding through the water in what used to be the backyard. You yelled, "Don't give up!" and you got a "Fuck you, stupid bitch!" back in response. Echoes. The world is all about echoes. Give the world the best you have and what comes back to you? What circles round? Why, you get kicked in the teeth. *Give the world the best you have anyway.*

On board the chopper that rescued you from the roof was an EMT who fashioned a makeshift tourniquet for your arm. They took you to a hospital and gave you treatment. They told you that you were one of the lucky ones. Ha!

51

You're not sure if it's a few days or a week or a few weeks later that you find your way back to Lou's house. You have to take a small boat and row it your damn self. Everyone thinks you're a ghost. Time is a crimson-vermilion paint stroke blurred and matted and bumpy on a sunken canvas and you miss Gauguin.

Alone.

You miss Lou and your fractious fantasies about him. You actually smile as you think about a common fantasy, touching him with both hands and not just a ghost hand, your lips swirling around his cock, hearing his moans, his breath coming back to touch you.

His mouth hard on yours. It seems more real than the wet and water everywhere, the flooded traffic sections, the Goliath limbs of felled trees, the reef of car and trucks roofs. You think of that writer, Virginia Woolf, who filled her pockets with stones and walked into the River Ouse. She was afraid of another psychotic break, of hearing voices. What a sad, sodden shame. Then you funnel your thoughts back to Lou. Desperate rescue workers lifting people off rooftops intrude. *I'm on the top of the world lookin' down on creation!*

You row until you're sitting before Lou's busted-up drenched half-burnt exploded house. There's something you need to do.

You grab a bag of tools you brought along, slide out into the water, haul the boat up on a ledge of earth, wade/swim back to the front of the house, hesitate a moment before the door, askew on its hinges, looking like it lost a fight with Leon Sphinx in his prime. You pray that you won't encounter anything slithery and poisonous in the dark, cold water you wade through.

The house you shared with Ray is almost completely gone. You feel weak. Good thing you are standing in water up to your waist, because otherwise you'd probably fall over.

And this is when you know full out you are a coward and a liar and a hesitater and a doubter. A wet, unemployed, homeless, should-be-dead, dirty, chronic masturbator with one hand. Don't think about this too much.

Don't think too much about how you were in love with Lou and never told him. He could probably see it in your eyes though, because you were never good at disguising your feelings. You were afraid. Afraid of Ray. Afraid of your feelings. Afraid of Lou. Afraid that he might love you back without you having used any magic tricks to make him do it.

When you are able, you go inside. There's still water and oily wet muck everywhere, mold and flies everywhere. The furniture is topsy-turvy like it's been on a Ferris wheel ride, wet-mold-disgusting smell everywhere, memories real and imagined, wet and dead now, the walls smeared with burn marks and a connivance of brown waterlines.

It's a strange time, really, to think about an escape Houdini did with beer in 1912. He did it in Scranton too in 1915. Houdini liked to do escapes that forced him to get out of confinement in water. But Houdini, who didn't drink, was easily overcome by the alcohol. He didn't, early on, realize the danger of the alcoholic substance and the fumes. At one performance in England, had it not been for his assistant, he might've drowned. He was only partially conscious when the assistant, unsettled by the quiet behind the curtain, dashed in and hauled Houdini out.

The lack of oxygen due to the carbonation of the beer made Houdini groggy and he nearly passed out and drowned. On that show a stagehand joked, "Why run away from the beer, Mr. Houdini? It's what most of us run after."

52

You head carefully up the slippery stairs, thinking about your lame escape from Katrina and the broken levees. You brace yourself as your eyes find Lou, still cuffed to the radiator, burned, drowned, his skin leathery, hardened. The water is no longer on the second floor.

You brought a hacksaw with you to cut him free. The hacksaw can cut through rope, wood, steel bars, small chains, and handcuffs.

Ladies and Gentlemen, watch now as my lame-ass, one-armed assistant attempts to cut through steel and wake a dead man to tell him she loves him!

You pull the hacksaw out of the bag like a magician pulls a rabbit from a hat.

You begin to saw the metal. You remember a trick the magician used to do, the magician you used to work for. The One Hand Cut. Kind of ironic to be thinking about that now too. The One Hand Cut is a method for cutting a deck of cards with only one hand. It's more a flourish. There's no real secret to doing it. All movements are in free view of the spectator and there's doubt as to how it's performed. It's simply a demonstration of dexterity. *Simply a demonstration of dexterity.*

Of which you have little now. You sweat. There's a reason police use handcuffs to prevent suspected criminals from escaping custody. Finally there is the clink and chomp of metal as you free Lou.

Then you notice the pitiful sound of dogs howling and moaning, whimpering from unseen windows.

You grab Lou by his sodden shirt collar, trying to ignore the unnatural coolness of his flesh, and somehow tow his stiff body down the mucky stairs. At one point, he slides against you, and you both fall down the stairs, his stiff body clunking along, pressing you under the water at the bottom. You flail about, finally get righted, drag his stinking corpse out the door and into the street, where he floats behind you like a great whale, and you pull him up on a patch of dry ground across the street below some family's blue shutters. *Boys don't last forever.*

Well, you used your whole body to more throw him than pull him. You're more of a thrower. *She storms out to the diamond, muscles in calves flexing rolling, the fans in the bleachers stomp and roar... she's a hefty girl... the wind-up the release the fast slap of ball against leather in catcher's mitt it's another strike... ladies and gentlemen, no one can hit her! She's spectacular!*

And the exasperated whale is purposing to spring clean over the craft, except the whale is dead and doesn't know it, and you are trying not to look at a statue in the yard of a cherub, all of it below the water except its eyes and the top of its head, trying not to feel like a cold pagan harpooner with her prize, finally disgusted by the way you've been abandoned. There are a lot of statues under water here....

53

The rain bitch-slaps your ass while you use your one hand to grip and then cover Lou's body with a ripped piece of tarp from an old boat. *Tat tat tat tat tat* is the sound of it against the tarp over his corpse, against your body. The rain is so hard it feels like someone is pelting you with a lot of little, stale gumballs. You know, the kind you get from a gumball machine for like a quarter or something.

Ray's house is practically gone, so you don't need to worry about him showing up and seeing you not being dead and all, and realizin' he failed at killing your ass. There aren't any police around either.

Concerned about the health implications of advancing decomposition, some people you don't know will later help you to bury Lou in a makeshift grave.

There wasn't any way to get a body taken to the morgue after Katrina. Morgues were full up anyway. Bloated corpses in blue jeans and T-shirts and sneakers were tied to trees, face down, in the water for later retrieval. If there was anything left of them after the animals got to 'em.

After Katrina

54

Sittin' in the stinky closet of Ray's new place, you had lots of time to think, think about girls in other states sunshine states who were in between in between in between semesters at college love affairs and marriage marriage and children marriage and children and divorce with their curved hips and skinny little waists and bright white smiles and smooth muscled thighs little to no cellulite perky breasts flat stomachs flat young dreams who aren't thinking beyond summer who are under water under water under water nonetheless but just don't know it yet who drive their shiny BMWs and Mercedes to the movies and to the malls shopping shopping buying stuff wondering "Will Daddy get me the midnight blue Mercedes this year?" and even your big red Caddy is premenstrual and bitchy and fucked in the heat. You and your car are both hormonal sex pots.

Willa Cather was right. At some point in life, the world just breaks in two. And if you're lucky, it happens during a Cat-5 hurricane, and you're suddenly manless homeless lopsided and writing bad checks for pet food and apparently haven't suffered enough and you're trying too hard and then you're not trying at all. You know, the illusion was never about a woman being sawed in half. It was about a woman holding herself *together.*

55

Hundreds of people are still unaccounted for in New Orleans. No one is sure how many. Some were probably washed into the Gulf of Mexico, the ninth largest body of water in the world. Some drowned when their boats and all their fishing gear sank. Some were pulled into Lake Pontchartrain or into swamps crawling with unpleasant and scary things like alligators and poisonous snakes. Some were buried under crushed and upended homes.

The levees broke. Failed. Erupted. Split. Fractured. Breached. Don't think about this too much. A mind all logic is like a knife blade.

You wonder how many statues are under water in this city, washed out into the Gulf of Mexico, sitting broken and regal on the bottom of the sea.

Maybe years from now they'll find statues of the Virgin Mary and street signs and Santa Claus and reindeer and ceramic pets, and maybe they'll find basketballs at the bottom of Lake Ponchartrain and jazz pianos and car parts all mixed together in a great stew with some gas lanterns and boats and barbecue grills and strollers and adding machines and headless statues of saints and wedding photo albums and volleyballs and wallets and soda bottles and chalkboards. Maybe.

You think about bent signs and twisted, broken trees and that picture of a chalkboard that someone posted two days after Katrina punched your city. Someone had scrawled:

We're sorry about the school but the shelter was a blessing. We had to bring over 150 people here. We got no help from any coast guard boats. People died and are still in their houses. THEY LEFT US HERE TO DIE. So we drew stars and air and dry land on the blackboard and prayed that we wouldn't be forgotten.

You sit in a Checkers fast food joint with your beloved grease and salt, wondering if Mary will show. You think of the ghost-like chalk scribbled in moments of desperation in that airless school. You think about how people need to express themselves or they'll go crazy. About how sometimes they express themselves and go crazy anyway. About how you wanted to give Mary time to get used to the idea that you weren't really dead, so you wrote and sent the letter last week and told her to meet you here, today, at lunchtime.

You think about the pale ghost of Van Gogh's face, how it keeps peering at you from the past and you bite into your double cheeseburger and wonder how Mary felt when she got your letter. She's the only one you really missed from your old life and the only one you ever really trusted.

Would she think the letter was some sort of sick prank?

You're not really a ghost but you might as well be one. You still haven't finished with Ray and you have no desire to return to your old, uninspired, crybaby life before you see justice done.

You want Mary to know you're still alive; you think she deserves that. Even though they only found your stupid left hand after the storm and even though they had a funeral for you and even though you like being a ghost and ironically feel more alive than you ever have. You still think she deserves to know.

You don't want or need to make a big deal out of still being alive. Because your old story had no ending.

You feel someone's eyes on you and look up. It's Mary. She's a sight for sore eyes in her sandals and white tank top and mauve shorts and sparkling, dangling silver earrings.

"Lordy," she says, smiling to the high heavens. She hugs you for a long time and then sits down with you.

To thank her for giving you such a nice send off into the afterlife, you buy her lunch. A large Coke, famously seasoned Checkers fries, and a double cheeseburger. You even spring for dessert for the both of you: banana-flavored milkshakes.

You don't know if it's the salt and fat or the grease and sugar, but you start talking and you can't stop. You tell her everything. You start from the beginning. You tell her about Ray. About Lou. About having to cut your own hand off. About coming back to haunt Ray, which you still aren't finished with because he's a murderer. You finally say it out loud. *He killed Lou and he tried to kill me.*

Mary listens with the patience of a saint while she chews her greasy beef and sips her milkshake and looks like she's memorizing your face.

You tell her about Matt, how you met the man you're sure will become your fifth husband by knocking him down in front of a soup kitchen. She laughs and the Heavenly Waters are constellations in her eyes.

You tell her about how you rowed out to Lou's house and drug his body outta there yourself. These days, not everybody can afford cadaver-sniffing dogs.

You talk about how you read, months after the storm, about family members, scattered across the country, calling hospitals, the Red Cross and missing persons hot lines, hoping their loved ones had been rescued.

Even though you know Mary knows all about the pink, grubby heartache that is New Orleans, you talk about how Grandmoms lay under couches moldering for months in their nightgowns and robes and slippers until someone found them the next spring. How bodies were impolitely wedged in piles of rubble, dangled from rafters or were face down, arms outstretched on parlor floors, many of them overlooked in initial searches.

You talk about the grotesque images of bodies left in plain sight. About how officials in Louisiana recovered more than 1,200 bodies, but the recovery process was hamstrung by money shortages and red tape.

"You see why I don't wanna make no big deal outta being a ghost, Mary? About being dead?"

She shakes her head. She does.

You think about how a few months after Katrina, the special operations team of the New Orleans Fire Department searched the Lower Ninth Ward for remains until they ran out of overtime money.

People always running outta things in the city.

Half a dozen FEMA officials refused to pay the bill. The media said it was because the required paperwork hadn't been filed.

In February 2006, FEMA agreed to pay for the search for bodies to resume, and on March 2 the agency's special operations team began a systematic check of the 1,700 structures in the Lower Ninth Ward — 1,700 — the site of the city's worst destruction.

Each team of firefighters worked with one or two dogs trained to find human remains. If the dogs sensed a body, the workers lifted heavy furniture, dug through stanky ass mud or pulled down ceiling tiles to find it.

"See Mary, I couldn't wait for no FEMA to get their act together and search for Lou's body and besides I knew where it was. I did what I had to do. Lou didn't have family nearby. They're all in Texas. I sent them a letter. I didn't know what else to do. And the police sure weren't going to help."

"You need any help with Ray, you just say the word," Mary says. "I never did like him."

You smile. Finish your burger. Burp. Quote Alfred Hitchcock. "Revenge is sweet and not fattening. Hitchcock said that. I appreciate that you wanna help, Mary, but this is something I gotta do myself." You think Van Gogh, who lived in a yellow house and painted 70 canvases in the last 70 days of his life, would've liked cheeseburgers.

You tell Mary about how Van Gogh, or you when you were Van Gogh, probably had something called temporal lobe epilepsy. It made you see ghosts and hear voices sometimes.

Isn't that ironic? Considering you are a ghost in your own life now.

When you were Van Gogh, you didn't have the grand mal seizures but you had terrible psychotic episodes and blanked out almost entirely when they happened. Didn't help that you were depressive, had syphilis, and were spastically lonely. And that you drank absinthe and methylated spirits from oil lamps.

"Mary," you say. "I've been trying to get people to *see* me for over a hundred years. To hear me. To connect with me. You were the best friend I ever had. One of the few who did see me. And yet you are still my friend." Mary laughs.

Later, when Mary leaves Checkers having promised to keep your secret, she's a beautiful, moving strobe of living colors... an honest, muscular wave of brown, mauve, and silver. If you have one good friend in life, well, that's something.

Ironically, you think about how Van Gogh's paintings, or your paintings when you were Van Gogh, contained no ghosts or visions or hallucinations.

You don't kid yourself that much has changed since 1890, when Van Gogh, or you, were done with society. You're all too familiar with the present-day lechery, disorder, delirium, madness, dishonesty, hypocrisy, shallowness, and general sordid contempt for anything that's unique or different. You've long known that the world lacks imagination.

You're glad that when you were Van Gogh you attacked the conformity of institutions. I mean, look what they did to you, those institutions. Look what they are doing to people today. Van Gogh, or you when you were Van Gogh, was ahead of his time in so many ways. His friend Albert Aurier, a friend and critic, once claimed that the fixed idea that haunted Vincent's brain was of the coming of a man, a messiah, a sower of truth, who would regenerate our decadent and perhaps imbecilic industrial society.

Your friend Gauguin thought the artist should look for the symbol and the myth and expand everything in life into a myth. You didn't. You believed we must know how to infer the myth from the everyday things in life.

You are brought out of your 1800s reverie by the smell of burning bananas. You smelled them when Katrina hit and split everything wide open, when you were trapped in that house.

One of the Checkers minimum-wage employees yells, "Damn milkshake machine!"

That's your cue to get up and leave.

You remind yourself that no one has ever written, painted, sculpted, or created anything except to extricate him or herself from some kind of hell.

Outside, looking at a still busted-up New Orleans, you know as a painter you rearranged nature. You know as a painter that you'll keep doing it. You'll keep throwing heaps of paint onto canvases, slashing and dotting, no matter what.

Van Gogh, or you when you were Van Gogh, once said, "I break through, I lose again, I examine, I grip hold of, I loosen, my dead life conceals nothing, and, besides, *le néant* has never done any harm to anyone, and what forces me to return to it is this distressing sense of absence, which passes by and sometimes drowns me, but I see very clearly into it; and I even know what *le néant* is, and I could tell you what is in it."

Le néant means nothingness.

You walk into the sun at two o'clock in the afternoon knowing your bad habits have shaped you as much as your good ones. And like a tidal surge, you head toward Ray's, determined to somehow finish this.

56

At some point, the world shifts. It shifts and there ain't squat you can do about it. You're surprised when you arrive at Ray's to do some big, bad-ass haunting and find out he's been delivered a little unexpected Newton's law of gravity.

You stand among Ray's neighbors, none of whom know you here, and listen to them recount the details of his ignoble death by toilet.

Just as he was walking beneath the tree with the toilet wedged in it, the large branch holding the toilet broke, and both the branch and the toilet fell right outta the tree, right on his stupid square block of a head. He died about an hour after the bizarre accident.

It's not nice, but you get that horrible feeling, like when you're in church and it's all quiet and you start thinking about laughing, and then you can't stop thinking about it, and then you know you're gonna full out laugh hysterically and everyone's gonna look at you and there's not a damn thing you can do about it.

"At least no one was using the toilet at the time," you say. Which gets you more than a few odd looks. You look at it as a little porcelain justice. Then you start laughing. And you truly can't stop.

As you drive your red, bloated Caddy through the rain-darkened streets of New Orleans, a big grin spreads across your face.

You think about how maybe being dead is no easier than being alive after all.   And when you get home, and tell Buttercup what happened, you start laughing again, thinking about how that dumb bitch Ray was killed by a toilet falling outta a Goddamn tree, and I mean, what are the odds of that? "Justice doesn't take no naps," you say to Buttercup between laughs and great gulps of air.   "Uh uh, justice doesn't take no damn naps."

57

You are watering the single plant in your rundown shack when you hear a knock on your door.

You open it and Matt stands there. "I don't care what you've done or haven't done or where you've been, or who you've been with. I don't care about your scars or your past or your missing hand or the fact that you think you were Van Gogh. I'd just like to love you and live for a while like we used to, you know, before Katrina," he says. "Before the levees broke."

You cry. He cries. You both cry and cry. Slowly your tears dry. The sound of water lapping at your heels slowly recedes and you drop the pitcher of water... finally let go of Lou's hand.

You put a CD into your cheap CD player. Fats Waller sounds spark into the night...

> *There's honey on the moon tonight*
> *A sin if we waste it*
> *Come along and let's taste it*
> *Had it ordered for you....*

What breaks and tears in you? Sinew, some bone-fragile memories of your inglorious past, a few big, old, sloppy life beliefs, and you are two more orphans of the storm. Actually, three with Buttercup. It ends a better night than most, better than you've had in a long time. You kiss all night, you and

Matt, and he holds you all night, and there's nothing apologetic about his wet tongue.

You finally fall asleep, Buttercup curled at your feet, your feet entwined with Matt's. You dream of a room fat and humming with the growl of a working air conditioner and not just a fan and watch as one by one, lights are turned on again all over your City Below the Sea.

It starts to rain.

58

When you are old, getting by in a nursing home, you get a visitor. He says his name is Troy. You don't think you know him. "Who did you say you were?"

"Troy." He shows you his art. Something inside you aches. You remember a Yellow House. Thirty or so normally decorous townspeople climbing it, all the way to its mustard windows, screaming cuss words in French, calling you a bastard, a lecherous soul, a fraud, a child snatcher, a molester of women. Yelling lies. Their spittled lips moving with art and fear. Then they were locking you away in an asylum.

You painted sunflowers then. You think. Lots of faces. Lots of hands and faces. Peasants and seascapes and portraits and almond blossom trees, the last year of your life smearing together.

Some potatoes.

Even though you only have one hand, your not-arm aches with the memory of painting canvases, portraits, cypresses, stars, and wheat fields. Trying to paint away all the doubts of yourself. Trying to connect all the echoes into a sound with meaning. Trying to forget all the boiled potatoes you ate, all the methylated spirits you drank.

The young man tells you something about a mural you painted a long time ago, on the side of a house in this city, a house with a tree growing in it, how you changed his life. He shows you a newspaper article about his art exhibitions in New York and LA and New Orleans.

Little statues march frozenly across the top of your TV. The Virgin Mary. Little animals. Bunnies. Dogs. Jesus. The Hindu goddess with four arms. You must've collected them for a reason, but you can't remember why now.

"You told me maybe it was our job to make things better," the man named Troy said. He has a tattoo etched on his right upper arm that reads: "RIP Lower Ninth."

"You painted the mural in this photo." He hands it to you and you look at it, the fingers on your one hand and your eyes caressing it.

"I said that?" you say. "I painted that? I mean, look at me, I have one hand. How in the hell could I have painted that?"

"You did."

There are times in New Orleans when everything you think you know suddenly shifts or gets turned topsy-turvy.

"You painted a lot of murals, Katrina. You don't remember?"

You shake your head no. The nurses in their crisp white uniforms with their squeaky shoes moving up and down the hallways give you a lot of medicine. Morphine mostly. Sometimes, at your age, it does funny things to you. Once you thought there were wild turkeys in your bed. Turkeys that were completely white, like chickens. You saw them clear as day. Sittin' there, gobbling at the end of your bed. What the hell? Another time, you thought you saw an art exhibit outside your window, a dozen impaled mannequin heads on pieces of wood, staring at you with their plastic, unmoving lips and eyes. Damn straight you liked the turkeys better.

You tell Troy hundreds of people are still unaccounted for in New Orleans. No one is sure how many. Some were probably washed into the Gulf of Mexico, the ninth largest body of water in the world. "Some drowned when their boats and all their fishing gear sank. Some were pulled into Lake Pontchartrain or into swamps crawling with unpleasant and scary things like alligators and poisonous snakes. Some were buried under crushed and upended homes. Some waited on rooftops and some got rescued by helicopters. A whole lot didn't."

You tell him the levees broke. Failed. Erupted. Split. Fractured. Breached. Don't think about this too much. A mind all logic is like a knife blade.

Where's the magic? "I wonder how many statues are under water in this city, in the Gulf of Mexico," you say. He sits down to listen to you. You haven't had a visitor in a long time. Your fifth and best husband, Matt, died last year.

"Maybe years from now they'll find statues of the Virgin Mary and street signs and Santa Claus and reindeer and ceramic pets, and maybe they'll find basketballs at the bottom of Lake Ponchartrain and jazz pianos and car parts all mixed together in a great stew with some gas lanterns and boats and barbecue grills and strollers and adding machines and headless statues of saints and wedding photo albums and volleyballs and wallets and soda bottles and chalkboards. Maybe."

Troy sketches you while you talk. Without looking up, he says, "You know that mural you painted? It's still there. I made sure to take care of it all these years. I take my kids to see it. I want them to know about what we went through. Those two trees that are part of the mural are still alive."

You look out the window. There are no unsmiling mannequins today. No white turkeys either. A tear slides down your cheek. You don't need to be Van Gogh anymore. You've forgiven yourself for that lifetime. You've helped the world forgive him, forgive you, for what you did to yourself. His last words, your last words in that lifetime, were *"La tristesse durera toujours,"* French for "Sadness will last forever."

The Auberge Ravoux, in Auvers-sur-Oise, where Van Gogh, or you when you were Van Gogh, spent his final months and where he died, is now a restaurant. People have lunch where you died and the ambiance is pretty good.

The waitresses set out country casseroles and crocks of pickles. You can order leg of lamb, pig's feet and oxtail, or chicken braised in cream. Auberge guests can then climb a set of creaking stairs and step into Van Gogh's, or your, old room, where he, or you, slept with many of your most famous paintings haphazardly piled under your bed. Then the guests can go next door and sit through a short sound and slide show.

Mental problems afflicted him, or you, particularly in the last few years of his, or your, life. During some of these periods you didn't paint, you weren't allowed to. Over one-hundred-and-fifty psychiatrists have attempted to label his, or your, illness, and some thirty different diagnoses have been suggested. This kind of cracks you up. That no one can definitively figure it, or you, out.

You look again at the statues marching across your TV. "My favorite is the one with four arms," you say.

There are things written on this city, on the front doors, the shutters, the bus terminals, the boats, the bars, the steamy streets, the banana trees, that only you can see.

"You saved me from a life of crime when I was a teenager," Troy says. You can see he is sketching your face. "I was a tagger. I spray-painted graffiti on stuff. I spray-painted foul language all over your mural and you forgave me. Instead of sending me off to the police, you gave me a paintbrush."

"I did?"

"It was like you hit me over the head with a drum mallet, but in a good way." He laughed. "You taught me about the history of graffiti, about graffiti artists who became famous and put their skills into creating art instead of defacing things. Now I'm a father with grown children." He pauses to pull pictures of their brown, smiling faces from his wallet, shows them to you, and re-pockets them.

Then he's back to moving his pencil with sure strokes, outlining and shading, creating your face.

"You know I went to my own funeral?" you say. And then the whole story comes pouring outta you while he continues to fill in your face and listen. You remember something about another woman's face looking out from beneath a painting of a patch of grass at the lime-yellow world.

You tell him how you, sitting there now with your old, sorry, used-up bones, used to be a failed hooker, a hotel maid, a magician's assistant in the Quarter, how you drove an ice cream truck for a while. How you used to be Van Gogh. He doesn't flinch. He wants to know about your hand because apparently you never told him what happened to it when he first met you, but why talk about something that's lost?

Soon it will be Springtime in New Orleans. Orchards will pop with peach blossoms and the bright cold will be gone.

You tell him how you used to sit in church, but never when it was full of people, how you loved this one greasy chicken joint that got clocked and bashed-up by a flying yacht during Katrina, about Matt, about Buttercup, about how your fourth husband was killed by a toilet falling out of a tree, and you slap your thigh and laugh, then turn serious again as you tell him about how your hair turned instantly white the night Matt passed away in his sleep. Matt, the love of your life. Someone you didn't expect to find. Someone who made you believe in magic again. And kisses. And moonlight. And backrubs. In art. In *life*.

In the shattered wet world outside.

You are surprised to find yourself believing forever in the artists to come.

Troy's lean fingers move the whole time across the paper, catching you, filling you, shading and nudging you into being. He holds it up. "What do you think?"

You stare at it. For the first time you are seeing yourself as you truly are. "Not bad. Not bad at all," you sniffle, remembering a wash of canvases and a faded woman.

You think about how you, as Van Gogh, painted more than thirty self-portraits between 1886 and 1889 and you never saw one as good as this.

You go back to looking out the window, seduced by the sound of his pencil scratching across the paper. "I'll need ten more tubes of zinc white," you say. You don't think he hears you. That's how it should be while a pencil or a paintbrush is stroking paper. You sit in silence for a while.

"I wonder who I'll be next?" you say.

He hands you the sketch. "There. You keep it."

You look at him confused. "Can I borrow your pencil?" He hands it to you. You write, painfully, slowly. Hand it back to him. "It's wonderful," you say. "But it belongs with you." He looks down at what you've written and smiles.

> *A handshake.*
>> *Yours,*
>>> *Vincent.*

"Perhaps Gauguin and I will work together again," you say as he's leaving and someone down the hall drops something, a dish plate, a glass, something, and it shatters. Outside the window, the wet sky with its Socrates-grey beard of clouds stares at you like you're an idiot but you finally understand it's afraid of *you,* the passionate painter who dares....

Somewhere, a kerosene lamp sputters, burns bluely, and goes out....

The End

ABOUT THE AUTHOR

Kelly Jameson has published fiction in many genres, including romance, mystery, suspense, humor and short fiction. *What Remained of Katrina* is her first novel to go beyond the bounds of genre into the realm of bold literary fiction. Among her other published titles are ***Dead On*** (film-optioned suspense/thriller), ***Shards of Summer*** (noir suspense), ***To Tame a Rogue*** (romance), and ***Desperate, Disturbed, Deranged & Double-Latté*** (short fiction). Her most recent success has been the best-selling **Hot Highlands Romance** series that includes ***Spellbound*** and ***Across a Dark Highland Shore***. For more information on these and other Kelly Jameson titles, please visit her website at www.keljameson.com. She lives with her family in Pennsylvania.

www.ingramcontent.com/pod-product-compliance
Lightning Source LLC
Chambersburg PA
CBHW032010170626
46807CB00006B/2730